I Will Shout Your Name

I Will Shout Your Name

Stories

John Matthew Fox

Press 53
Winston-Salem

Press 53, LLC
PO Box 30314
Winston-Salem, NC 27130

First Edition

Cover design by Alicia Kleman
www.aliciaklemanart.com

Author photo by Amber Fox

Library of Congress Control Number
2017954778

Printed on acid-free paper
ISBN 978-1-941209-65-3

For my wife Amber,
whose love for art sustains my writing

Grateful thanks to the editors of the publications listed below for first publishing the following stories:

Chicago Tribune, "The Descent of Punch the Frog" (Finalist, Nelson Algren Award)

Crazyhorse, "Down on the Pitch"

Prime Number Magazine, "Tentmaking in Tehran"

Shenandoah, "To Will One Thing" (Winner, The Shenandoah Prize for Fiction)

Third Coast, "Fatu Ma Futi" (Winner, Third Coast Fiction Contest)

Contents

Fatu Ma Futi

When I walked off the tarmac into luggage claim, Tanielu was waiting in old sandals and a flower-print shirt that hung like a bell over his lavalava. He threw leis around my neck. Though we only recognized each other from emailed pictures, we hugged. On the drive along the only road of the island, he spoke about plans for the school as I watched the waves stumble over the distant reef and glide into the coral shore. I would enjoy the kids, he told me. And the builders had almost finished constructing the new schoolhouse where I would be teaching. His speech bore markers I'd soon recognize as Samoan, but were exaggerated in him: unhurried, self-assured, and unwilling to speak more than necessary.

His house sat on the same property as the old school building, a thatched-roof room with three open walls. The new schoolhouse, a two-story concrete-block construction, towered next to it. The whole lot was on a graveyard of coral: porous, lightweight, and abrasive. Under my feet it grated, with a slight harmonic tone. But the view astonished me most. Thirty yards offshore, still in the shallows, just before the reef, a massive rock spurted up into the sky. On its top grew smatterings of shrubs and grass.

"Fatu Ma Futi," Tanielu said.

"If I ever get lost, I can just look for that," I joked.

"You can't get lost here," he said. "You either follow the road left or right."

Over the next week, I prepared for the subjects of Math (or Maths, as Tanielu said), English, and Bible. My mother's rigorous homeschooling had prepared me for all three, and in my recent college studies, I'd majored in the third. Since this was ministry, I'd only be paid in room and board, but my true reward was elsewhere. Sina, Tanielu's wife, always shooed me out of the kitchen and prepared moist tuna sandwiches— "Samoan Tuna," she bragged—adding hefty amounts of mayonnaise to the already oil-saturated fish. Though she was much shorter than her husband, she carried nearly as much weight. Sometimes she delighted me and other times intimidated me—she could switch from dimpled sweet to good-natured scolding with a mother's adroitness, even though she was not a mother. Tanielu and Sina were just past childbearing age, but childless, and I guessed they found comfort in spending time with the children at the school.

The day before the kids arrived, Tanielu and I drove to the grocer's to pick up some onions and coconut milk for Sina. Tanielu let me ride in the bed of the truck, where I lay on my back and watched the scrolling of the palm-tree strip of sky. At the grocer's, the shelves held food with shelf life long enough to survive the apocalypse, while one small section held fresh fruit and vegetables. Gnats swarmed like buzzards over the carcasses of blackening bananas.

After the grocer's I caught my first glimpse. As we left, in front of a nearby store, I saw the fafafine. I've only stared a few times in my life—at a man with a goiter on his neck the size of a cantaloupe, and at a female beggar in Los Angeles without arms or legs—but here I stared. I never wanted to stop looking, even though I knew I should. The fafafine towered over his conversational partner, with his heels adding four inches. Given his bulkiness, the stiletto support appeared miraculous, two slim steel beams propping up the skyscraper of his body. And his heftiness wasn't obesity, but the result of thick shoulders and thighs and chest and arms. An overwhelming amount of muscle gussied up in dainty apparel. When he turned his head to gesture at a rack of merchandise outside the store, his lips glistened and eyelashes shone with makeup. I initially thought he was wearing a lavalava, but since the fabric lacked a slit down the side, it was actually a plus-sized skirt. He spoke to a shopkeeper in a bass voice, which contrasted so sharply with his feminine accessories that it seemed ventriloquistic. I dropped one of the bags of food and picked it up hurriedly, hoping the sound hadn't attracted their attention. As I looked back, though, I caught the head of the fafafine already returning to the conversation. The thought that he had seen me tingled my fingertips.

I'd known the term fafafine from house chatter where I'd been taught all the important Samoan phrases for a teacher: *Salapu lou guku*, shut your mouth, *nofo ilalo*, sit down. When Tanielu mentioned fafafine, I asked the meaning. A lady-man, he said, laconic as always. Which was different than the homosexual Samoans, I knew: the tailor who'd custom-fitted my island-print shirts, putting the buttons on the left side even after I'd requested the right side, he was gay. Flamboyantly so, with wispy voice to boot. That was disconcerting. A lady-man was different. I'd heard many sermons on the evils of homosexuality, but none on cross-dressing.

Tanielu, waiting down the hall, called, "Nothing to see." I flinched, worried that the fafafine had heard. After we'd put the groceries in the truck bed, I climbed in the passenger's seat and Tanielu fiddled with the clutch until the engine hiccupped to life.

"Hadn't seen a fafafine yet?" Tanielu asked. I shook my head. "Surprised you," Tanielu said, and it sounded like an accusation.

"Did you know him?" I asked, belatedly wondering if the pronoun should be female.

"Second cousin. Not a good man." He gently curved around a beachhead.

In the face of Tanielu's disapproval, I wondered whether I'd been too eager. But he didn't pursue the point. We sat in silence until he flipped on the radio and used the gift of singing endowed to every Samoan to harmonize with an oldies song about strange things happening, but instead of accompanying him I turned to the ocean and closed my eyes and started imagining.

Every fifteen minutes, the island bus dropped off clusters of kids. They shot across the coral lot with the energy of comets, yet their lavalavas never loosened. I had to adjust mine frequently because I hadn't gotten the knack of how to wrap it. Tanielu suggested a bobby pin, but that seemed like cheating. At first I hadn't wanted to wear anything dress-like, but realized on this island, it was masculine.

The first day went moderately well. I only remembered the names of the twins because they were constantly misbehaving. The younger kids, amused by my pale freckled skin and red hair, poked me. During playtime, when boys kicked the partially deflated soccer ball across the coral and girls braided thread into spiraled strands, Sina lumbered up with a snack of crackers and tuna fish.

"How are they?" she asked.

"Exhausting," I said.

"The blessing of children!" she said, beaming out over the yard as if I'd just claimed they were a troop of angels. Then she turned on me. "Eat your food. You need strength."

In the afternoon, as the workers painted the other side of the building, the fumes drifted into our room. I wanted to close the windows, but the breeze fought the heat and humidity.

The fumes certainly didn't make the kids talkative. Every time I asked Pannielo whether he understood a math problem, he just hiked up his eyebrows. I repeated the question three times before I understood that the eyebrow raise was an answer. I guessed it meant yes. When he asked me a question back, I tried the eyebrow raise myself, but he didn't understand. Maybe my eyebrows could not speak proper Samoan.

Near the end of the day, I was leaning over a desk helping a girl with addition problems when the body filled the doorframe. Its girth blocked the light. In my peripheral vision, I recognized the fafafine, though I had no idea why he'd visit my classroom. Perhaps he was one of the painters? Or he had come to see me for some reason? I prepared to swivel to greet him, already considering my smile, whether to shape it generously or politely. But I held off, pretending not to notice, pretending to help the girl with one more problem. I finally decided I should act as if I'd never seen him before. Then we could properly meet and I could touch him through a handshake.

But when I swung up, my mouth already shaping a prim smile, it was not the fafafine at all. It was a swarthy man, his lavalava hiked up to his thighs. His body and clothing was speckled with paint. His elbows braced the door like Samson. I couldn't believe that I'd mistaken his silhouette for the fafafine—they didn't look anything alike. Too short, not as broad.

"Paint bothering you?" he asked.

I wondered why he'd waited until the end of class to ask, but all I said was, "Not at all." As he left, I offered a parting smile, but the corners of my mouth hiked up without any goodwill.

I woke on Saturday morning in a warm pudding of humidity. Through my window I could see Fatu Ma Futi. One of my older boys had joked about the rock: "Some say it's a man," pointing a finger from his crotch, "and some say it's a woman," tugging at his nipple. I told him that was inappropriate, but privately thought he'd gotten it right. A low fog draped across its top, but by the time I'd eaten a doughy breakfast of *pankeke*, the fog had burned off. I arrived at the soccer field at ten, the time for a scrimmage according to a man at church, and slathered on sunscreen. Though my mother had prodded me into playing in elementary school and junior high—she used her beauty to intimidate me into doing activities I normally wouldn't—I hadn't played since then.

I juggled the ball waiting for everyone. No one arrived. I got lonely, then self-conscious. Had I gotten the time wrong? Finally, at eleven fifteen, a pudgy Samoan showed. He assured me more people were coming. I remembered that I'd had to press the man at church for the exact time, and now realized why. This place ran on island time, not clock time. Which explained the school kids arriving an hour late without shame or apology.

Just before we started the game, he arrived. I saw him unfold out of the tiny bus, his shoulders brushing both sides of the exit. He wore regular men's clothes: mesh shorts, T-shirt with the sleeves cut off, sandals. He had huge biceps, and shoulder muscles like half a flowerpot. Apart from his size, he looked so normal in men's clothes. No one would ever guess his other habits.

The game was a flurry of limbs, but no one mule-kicked. Besides, everyone played barefoot. I enjoyed watching the locomotion of the huge Samoans. They powered up and started chugging, increasing speed until they blistered the grass, and then crushed the ball or smacked another player. I played fullback, although no positions were assigned. By complete coincidence, the fafafine played forward, which meant I had to defend him. I didn't know whether to play tough or easy. It was like when a girl snuck into a guy's pickup basketball game. No one wanted to guard her. Too much backing in, too much sharing of sweat, too much awkward friction. A guy's body was just a mass of flesh, unspecial, but some bodies were marked—every contact, no matter how brief, tingled.

During the first one-on-one encounter with the fafafine, I hovered away, not daring to press up against him, but he passed for a score. The next time we chased a loose ball, we slammed into one another, shoulders sparring for position. By weight alone, he displaced me. But I hassled him long enough that my teammate hurtled into the fray, chopping out my legs so that I crashed down. The three of us fell, flailing, in an orgy of limbs. Head brushed on chest, leg flush on leg, hair and smells and heavy breathing. The fafafine's sweat smeared onto my skin. He wasn't wearing deodorant. And then we were up and into the next stage of the game. "Why you'd fall?" my teammate asked me. A weird question, as if I'd had a choice.

The other team skunked us, six-to-two. My mother demanded better from me when I'd played on our homeschooler team. After the game, I pressed a forefinger against my skin, and the tone sunk to white before flushing pink. Sunburnt. My shins hurt from splints and my lungs hurt from the unfamiliarity with exercise. When the fafafine lumbered toward me, I inwardly cowered, but he stuck out a hand. "Farva," he said. His hand enveloped mine. It was shockingly hot.

"Jordan," I said.

"I'm glad you insisted on guarding me," he said. "You're good."

I didn't think I had insisted, but nodded to accept the compliment.

"What are you doing here in Samoa?" he asked.

When I told him about volunteering for the school, Farva immediately shouted, slapping a hand against his forehead. "My son is there. Aggara. You know him?"

Aggara. The name was briefly unfamiliar, as faces swung by like sheets on a line, but then I remembered. "Of course, yes, Aggara." Not a bad child, just unremarkable. "Good kid," I added, just to allay the man's fears.

"And how do you like Tanielu?" Farva asked, but when he said the name, his face tightened at the edges and his tone stiffened.

"Fine, fine. He keeps things running well."

"We know each other," Farva said, not happily. Then he phoned in a smile and clapped me on the back. "See you next Saturday," he said. It sounded like a promise to me, even though he might not have meant it that way. As he walked off, patches of earth depressing under his weight, I wondered about Aggara's mother.

At the school the following morning, I looked for Aggara. I knew the placement of his chair—far right, third row—better than I could recall his face. He chewed gum and swung his feet, scuffing the floor with his blue flip-flops. I saw the resemblance to his father. The nose in particular, the ridge between his eyes flattening out to the delta on his cheeks. As the rest of the class filtered in, I raised my head periodically from the desk to glance at Aggara. His home life must be rough. Even if he lived with his mother. And the kids must rib him for the fafafine connection. On an island, there's no escape from an embarrassing second cousin, much less your father.

After the lessons of English grammar, we went down to the wooden picnic tables of the former schoolhouse and ate sandwiches under its thatched roof. Afterwards, the kids played games in the dead coral yard. They could walk barefoot on it, because of leathery calluses, but it hurt me. Aggara played with a group of five boys. Boys took turns against the wall as other boys chucked a rubber ball at them. Points were awarded. Aggara appeared to be losing. He had none of his father's tenacity or size.

A ball bounced off a kid's head, Aggara was blamed, a scuffle started, with chests shoved and shirts seized and complaints shrilled. Tanielu waded into the mix and came out clutching Aggara's ear. Aggara winced, standing on his toes, his head angled diagonally.

"Stop," I said, and hurried over. "It wasn't his fault."

Tanielu stopped, but didn't let go of his ear. "He was fighting," he said, nodding down towards Aggara.

"They were picking on him," I said, lacking direct evidence. But fighting wasn't like Aggara. Tanielu stared at me long enough to make me feel we were in a standoff. Perhaps he felt odd that I would dare challenge his authority in front of the kids, but if he did, it never interrupted his placid expression. He let go of the boy's ear. Aggara moaned and rubbed it. Then Tanielu herded him back to the other boys and gave everyone a lecture about playing fairly. When Tanielu returned to the house, he didn't speak to me.

After lunch, it was time for Bible. Today's story came from the Old Testament, with Abraham preparing to sacrifice his son Isaac, only to find the ram as a substitute. I had no activity planned post-story, but as I finished, I decided to ask kids to share about their own fathers. I picked two kids before asking Aggara to share.

"My father works for the Americans," he said. I nodded, soliciting more. "When I stay with him, he takes me to the beach on the other side and we snorkel. Once a year we fly to the other island to visit relatives." Western Samoa, he meant. I prodded, but he didn't offer more. Two boys whispered in the back. I called on one to go next.

Afterwards I assigned everyone to write about when their fathers sacrificed something for them. Kids buried themselves in their paper, except for the few daydreamers. Aggara was one. He looked everywhere except at me. When I called him to the desk, he appeared alarmed. He wasn't the type to be called up. My voice verged on a whisper, to avoid disturbing the rest of the classroom. "I met your father," I said. He waited. "Playing soccer. He was very nice. Do you stay with him often?" His eyebrows rose. "How often?"

"Every Tuesday. Sometimes Wednesday." He twisted his body back and forth. In his little lavalava, he looked cute. His hands were clenched in front of him.

"And usually you live with your mother?" Eyebrows up.

"Where does your father live?"

"Near the petrol station."

I told him to return to his seat, and shuffled papers on my desk without looking at them. As he picked up his pen and bowed his head to the paper, I noticed for the first time how much his mouth also resembled his father's.

The preparation for the roast began early that morning, before I woke. Sina gutted a suckling pig and buried coals and wrapped the pig in banana leaves before lowering it into the pit and shoveling a layer of dirt on top. By the time Tanielu and I had returned from the Sunday service, where I'd tried to pray but my concentration kept wavering, she'd erected parallel concrete blocks, across which she lay mesh. Beneath, coals glowed. Above, chicken sizzled.

It was my first roast and they instructed me to dress nicely. To be polite, all the men served themselves first. Farva came late. Presumably he was welcome because his son attended the school. He wore a lavalava and plastic flip-flops, but his lips glistened with a colorless sheen. Tanielu left to help Sina when Farva came under the awning.

I located Farva a few minutes later. He was cutting meat on Aggara's plate. Another family came in and sat between myself and Farva and Aggara. The heat compelled me to move to the edge of the building, where the breeze was stronger, and I stopped focusing on them. While at the edge, I ate a chicken leg. Sina swished over and firmly told me that I was a bad example to the children. Rude to eat while standing. "And stop staring," she added, even though I hadn't been. A parent chatted to me about her daughter until she left for another helping. It was now into the second hour of the roast, and my belly was swollen.

I completely lost track of Farva and focused on eating pork and fish until my plate was clean and I had to go for seconds. Surprisingly, he was also at the food spread, seizing legs of chicken and roasted bananas. I hung back at first, not wanting to crowd him, but when he moved to one side, I stepped up and reached for the serving spoon in the cabbage. Just as I did so, he swung back to my side of the table and our shoulders collided. He excused himself, then recognized me. "Jordan," he said in his deep voice, clearly glad. He rested a hand on my shoulder and whispered conspiratorially, "Eat the *palusami* before it's gone. Sina makes it best."

I ate that plateful quickly and decided to go up to my room, in the old classrooms on the second floor. The hum of the fan drowned out the crowd's drone. Geckos scurried across the white walls. I lay on my bed and listened to the slower cycle of the fan beneath the steady whirring, the revolution between higher and lower pitches. The sheets felt damp against my skin, due to the rising heat, due to the closed door. I lay there for some time, moving only a little, imagining scenes of bare skin, before finishing and wiping and going to the window.

Down in the coral courtyard, between the old schoolhouse and the house, Farva and Tanielu faced off.

Farva was speaking, his hands rotating over each other, then spreading wide. Tanielu's arms were crossed, and his feet were planted wider than his shoulders. His lips were taut. At one point Farva pointed a finger toward Tanielu, and Tanielu eyed it as though ready to bite it off. When Tanielu spoke, he did not move, but his words caused Farva to roll his head exaggeratedly, then wag his index finger. The shape of his mouth and the way he tilted forward made me believe he was not speaking quietly. Sina, pot in hand, ducked between them like a referee and said a few words. They separated without looking at each other or shaking hands.

When I returned to the feast—which lasted another two hours—parents talked to me about their children. I told everyone their children were wonderful, even the father of the twins. At some point, Farva and Aggara must have slipped out, because they weren't in the main area or by the kitchens or near the bathrooms or by the classrooms or anywhere else.

That night I did not eat dinner. I told Sina I probably wouldn't need to eat for a month. She chuckled and waved a hand at me and said she'd fatten me up before I went back to Los Angeles. The three of us played cards and talked until the moon was high. Then I went up to the classrooms for bedtime, Sina following me up. She fingered my bedsheet and asked if I needed another. I told her no, and then she asked if I was too hot, because she could find me another fan. I said no again. As she left, asking me if I wanted the light flipped out (I didn't), I smiled out of one corner of my mouth at her. Sometimes she was too easygoing and compliant to be a mother.

"Sina," I said, and she stepped back in. "What were Tanielu and Farva arguing about?"

She sighed. "They were not arguing about their argument," she said. "You understand?"

I lowered my eyebrows, and she laughed.

"Listen," she said, "They argue about relatives, and money, and food, and weather. But they never argue about their disagreement."

"What's their disagreement?"

Sina put a hand on the side of the door. I could see her formulate how to tell me, or wonder how much she should tell me. "Listen," she said. "A fafafine belongs to the women. So a fafafine must sleep with the men. But…Aggara."

"Aggara," I said.

"So Aggara is a reminder. Of what Farva does. He is a swinging door. But enough." She prepared to leave, then stopped. "Do you claim a sweetheart? She must be missing you."

"No," I said. "No sweetheart back home." It had been a while since I had dated, since my college days, where the college wanted us to call it "courting." I loved women but lacked the bravery to ignite relationships.

"Ah," Sina said, waving her hand dismissively. "You will get one soon enough, handsome man you."

I waited until Wednesday. On Wednesday, Aggara wore the same lavalava that he'd worn on Tuesday, but not his bead bracelet. He hadn't sparred with the other boys since the incident, and I had completely ignored him. After class, the kids went down to the coral yard and slapped their book bags against their legs as they waited for the bus.

Tanielu sat at the kitchen table, glasses slung low on his nose, looking over bills while Sina kneaded breadfruit on the counter. I asked to borrow the truck.

"Where are you heading?" Tanielu asked.

"To the grocery store. For snacks."

Tanielu looked to the queue of kids. "You can't take the bus?"

"I might come back late."

"Bus runs until nine."

"I think I'd prefer to drive." That part was true. I enjoyed tamping my speed down, letting the air batter the open cabin. Much more pleasurable than the cramped bus, with the aisles blockaded with stumps of knees and the sticky metal floors.

Tanielu offered the keys, but as I left, he bowed his head and Sina kneaded thoughtfully, like parents waiting to discuss their troublesome son. I rumbled the truck's engine alive and pulled out to the asphalt, waiting for the line of kids to file on the bus. Yes, Aggara climbed in. I tracked his head as he trundled down the center aisle and took a seat on the right side, next to the bell cord that lets the driver know to stop.

The bus started jerkily, groaning through the gears. For cover, I created distance, far enough back that I only saw the bus during long, wide bends. The distance didn't help me to monitor Aggara, but let me avoid stopping every time the bus did. Twice, though, I came around a bend to find the bus stopped. I stopped, too. Right behind. An obvious mistake. I felt the coals of the driver's eyes burning through the rear view mirror.

Aggara's head remained in the window. I vaguely knew the area where he'd told me he lived, roughly fifteen minutes up the road. But I figured I should follow him just to make sure. When he scrambled off, I almost missed it. I had come around a curve to find the bus resuming its route from the shoulder, and didn't see his tiny frame until I passed. I braked and parked perpendicular to the road in a bed of deep sand. Jogging back to where Aggara had disembarked, I found him plodding along, shifting heavily from one foot to the other, his backpack dwarfing his frame. I quick-stepped to close the distance, though I wasn't going to say hello. Thankfully, Aggara didn't turn. He kicked at rocks on the road's shoulder. Once he stopped to yank a weed out of the ground. After a few lots, he turned in. I rounded the natural hedge to hear a deep voice greeting him.

This was the least planned part. Mostly, this stage had involved dreamy plots. I would knock, and Farva would be happy to see me. Or I would knock and explain how I wanted to check up on Aggara, and Farva would be happy to see me. Or I would knock and apologize for Tanielu's actions over the weekend, and Farva would be happy to see me. We would eat local olives and fresh fish marinated in a coconut sauce, and laugh the night away over a grand table. Aggara would sit by, silent as always, just enjoying our combined company. But now knocking on the door seemed presumptuous. I had no reasonable answer for how I had found the house, or why I hadn't just come home with Aggara.

I opted for surveillance. I circled the house on its far side, fighting through the underbrush, trying to do so quietly without success. Red fruit, the size of plums, hung in clusters. From my new vantage, I saw the open porch in back. Aggara sat on a wooden table, picking splinters off the surface. His father, out of sight, scraped metal on metal. They talked, and though I remained completely still, I couldn't hear. Day fell. Sunset blushed across the sky. My legs cramped and I shifted them. Aggara and his father were eating now, heaping platefuls of food that smelled like fish and vegetables and potatoes all stirred into one. My stomach growled. When they finished, they went inside, and I had no way to see them. I edged over so I could look in a window.

As they sat on the couch, Farva read to his son. It looked like an after-dinner tradition. I'd assumed a more dysfunctional situation, between split parents and a cross-dressing father, but this seemed quaint and cute. Something tickled across my neck, and I slapped at it. Just a branch. Hiding out here, among the trees, reminded me of one time when I'd hid from my mother in the fir trees adjacent to our house. I hadn't committed any of the infractions on her refrigerator list, but I was tired of being bullied, tired of being required to jump whenever she called me. My independence reared. She came around beating the branches with a stick. When she found me, she told me never to do that again. After that, it felt like she wouldn't let me out of her sight for years. She was the most domineering woman I'd ever known.

I heard movement, but didn't realize Farva was coming until he rounded the corner with the trash bag in hand. The shadows hid his face but his frame loomed large. Heat pulsed off him. At first, I don't think he noticed me, but then I stepped on a branch. His whole frame tensed. His silhouette, framed by the porch light, bristled.

"Who is that?" he said.

"It's me," I squeaked. "Jordan. Aggara's teacher." My throat constricted. I couldn't get air in or fully formed words out. I fought my way out of the bushes and stood before him. Backlit by the porch light, he was beautiful but intimidating.

His body slumped. "Oh," he said. "What are you doing here?"

"Just came by to check on Aggara." It was the first lie that seemed plausible.

Farva switched the trashbag to his other hand, as if freeing his right for a swing. He seemed to be thinking about my response. "No you weren't," he said. "Why did you come?"

I had thought he'd be polite, at least. Accept my obviously faulty explanation on face value, and we could sit down and talk and later I could make up something else.

"To see your place," I said.

He paused, as if knowing this also was a lie, but waved a hand behind him. "So does it impress you?" he asked.

I offered the truth: "It's nicer than I thought it would be."

He twisted to the tin trashcans and threw the bag inside. The lid clanged back down. "Well, do you want to come inside?" he said, rubbing his hands together quickly.

"No, I couldn't," I said. "No." My fantasies now seemed thin and unbelievable.

Farva shook his head. "You are a runner," he said. "First time I saw you on the field, I thought: this boy is a runner, not a fighter."

Aggara appeared behind him. Side by side, it was such a contrast. I smiled at him, weakly. When I tried to say hello, my throat latched shut.

"Aggara says you've been very nice to him the last couple of days," Farva said.

I offered a nod, squirming. "I have to go now." I didn't look at either of them as I left. My body tensed, lowering my head slightly as if expecting a blow, listening for footsteps.

"Come back when you're ready," Farva said as I reached the road, but I didn't dare look behind.

I walked toward the main road, my heart double thumping. Via island talk, would this swing back to Tanielu? I had no easy explanations for why I needed the truck or why the grocery store turned into Farva's yard. I was suddenly struck by the sight of my arm—the dense pattern of freckles and the prairie-like bowing of hair. It seemed infinitely strange and not my own.

Back at the road, I tried to back the truck out, but the tires spun and ate half-moons into the sand. Lots of sand spitting, but no movement. Bald rubber. I tried to dislodge the vehicle by going forward, which rocked me out, but the tires quickly dug in again. I grabbed the keys and left. Maybe if I caught a ride back, Tanielu could help me solve things.

The porch lights of the neighbors shone into the darkness. A chicken clucked; waves murmured ashore. My head spun, feeling light. My ears hurt. I suddenly couldn't remember which way to go. One road around the island, and I couldn't remember which way was closer: left or right? Which way was Fatu Ma Futi? It should have been the easiest choice, but all my equilibrium had leaked out. The stars wheeled and the reef seemed unmoored. I'd flag down the first car that came, I thought, I'd hitch a ride in whatever swung my way. Just as I'd decided, headlights from both directions began to brighten the asphalt.

The Descent of Punch the Frog

Amy spoke to her husband in numbers. Sometimes she waited until he prompted her: "How many?" He did not say the word, as though if he refused to embody it in words it could not haunt the body of his son. She kept a daily tally so the doctors could adjust Aiden's dosages, making scratches in series of five on their chalkboard. She didn't tell Derrick when she might have miscounted. They had a contract—he would slave away at oil safety so they could afford the high insurance premiums and drugs shipped from Canada, and she would care for Aiden. Most of the time she felt wholly inept at her part of the deal.

She cooked dinner as Aiden showed his father the elbow scratch he'd received from falling during one of his episodes, and Derrick played lion with him in the living room, blowing against his stomach and tickling his armpits. At the dinner table she struggled to get Aiden to finish all his vegetables and pudding. The pills were in the pudding, which she thought sounded like the ominous cousin of a common saying. Their pill collection grew monthly, the orange canisters of varying heights studding the kitchen counter like organ pipes. During dinner, Derrick asked her to refill his water glass twice, and she did it even though, while she was gone, Aiden spilled his bowl. When Derrick asked her about Aiden's day, Amy spelled out the negative words to shield them from her child.

At bedtime she heard Derrick reading *Punch the Frog* to Aiden. Aiden loved that book, which Amy had found at an estate sale in South Pasadena and would have thrown away after the first reading except Aiden begged to hear it every night. It was too strange for a children's book. She only caught patches as she crisscrossed the house cleaning up discarded toys, but she knew the book so well that the house seemed to be reciting it in stereo. Derrick was at the beginning, when Punch the Frog wakes up to find his neighbors, Rabbit, Turtle and Squirrel, pounding on his door. When he opens the door, his lips crusty with last night's meal of flies, they accuse him of being a bad frog, a terrible animal. Punch the Frog is confused. He proclaims his innocence. He asks what he's done. When they simply repeat the vague accusations and demand that he suffer, he retreats into his house and cries big frog tears, their protests still audible through the mud walls. He can think of nothing he has done that would deserve such punishment. The next day they continue to harass him, until Punch flees his house and hides by the lake. While he's hiding there, he watches Rabbit, trying to escape from a preying eagle, fall in the lake and begin to drown, so Punch dives to rescue her.

Derrick stopped the story. He stopped for too long, longer than the turn of a page. Amy listened until Derrick said in a voice straining to be calm, "It's a bad one."

They formed a shell around their child, whose body jolted from an unknown electricity. Aiden's eyes explored the top of his sockets and the bones of his back arched like wings unable to sprout. Waiting out his tremors felt like waiting out a war. Her husband smelled of burnt tar and failing deodorant, and Amy inhaled it deeply because it smelled exactly like him and because she had not focused on that smell for some time. She was surprised to find that Derrick's face, viewed this close, seemed foreign to her, like the landscape of some lunar surface she had just discovered. The fault lines at his eyes creased and smoothed, and she noticed new lines, or ones she had not seen before. Derrick studied her face and seemed disappointed. She tried to summon up an expression such as anguish—anything that would reassure him that she could give form to the appropriate emotions—but her face failed her. Aiden continued to shake.

The book was open to the most terrifying page, one depicting murky fronds around a large, black hole of water. It was the type of hole that frogs and people fell into and could not escape. Frog had to enter that hole to do battle for the life of Rabbit. Amy never looked at that page too long. By a trick of lines and angles, it collapsed the world into itself. Once, on a day when she told Derrick far too high a number, she had reached that page and could read no further.

Aiden surfaced, his body under control again. "Your neck okay?" she asked. She patted his shoulder the way a coach would. He blinked, teetering between emotions. A spot of blood stained his lip and she quickly wiped it away. "You're fine," she said. By the time she returned with his nighttime glass of coconut water, the book had been forgotten and Derrick was making Aiden laugh by imitating a monkey. Aiden had returned to them, as he always did, as a normal child, but it was always a temporary return, as if he did not hold citizenship in the realm of the healthy and suffered periodic tests to renew his visa.

She already knew what would happen. Derrick would look at her with plaintive eyes, the same ones that cajoled her into saying yes after only seven months of dating and yes to trying to get pregnant immediately, and say that another night in their bed couldn't hurt. Yes, Aiden would occupy the space that separated them, the space they crossed less and less. Derrick would read his history of the Korean War and she would read selections from her anthology of love essays, and when Aiden began to tremble they would both reach out to comfort him. If he had another bad episode, they would turn to their sides and link their arms over him like a lattice. Derrick would sleep, waking only for Aiden's worst episodes before immediately falling back to rest, while she would lie awake exhausted, snatching patches of shut-eye that never added up to the sum of their parts. The bed would feel like the ridge of a fence. She would misinterpret every twitch from Derrick or Aiden as the initial shudders of yet another attack. And in the empty hours crawling toward dawn, she would clutch the frail body of her spasming child for the fifth or tenth or twelfth time and rediscover in his flesh the evidence of how powerless she was.

Aiden's first episode had occurred on his second birthday. It had been so petite: a fluttering of eyelids, a blip of interruption. Still, it worried Amy. She revisited the fears of her pregnancy: that she had deprived her son of nutrients, that the half-cooked egg or sips of wine had tweaked his brain. He hadn't been an easy child in the early years, refusing to latch onto her breast and losing a dangerous amount of weight, which forced her to feed him via syringe. All those fears mushroomed when the episodes grew more frequent and intense. Doctors, so many doctors, in hospitals, so many hospitals, prescribed cocktails of unpronounceable drugs and gave contradictory advice. This was when Amy was finishing up a low-residency graduate degree in painting, and looking back at her work from that time she noticed a gradual change from the elegance of long strokes to sharp, jagged slashes, as if her own hand had developed a sympathy for her son's state.

Twice, Aiden had stayed overnight at the hospital, lying on a bed in a soundproof room. Wires ran from his head like he was generating power. Computers recorded charges racing through lobes, colors flaring across his brain like the northern lights. As the doctors studied series of images, perplexed by the way the location hopscotched, Amy and Derrick waited outside the one-way glass, sipping burnt coffee from Styrofoam cups, looking away when their child cried out for them in his sleep.

The drugs had escalated. First a double dose failed, and a triple dose, and even a quadruple dose, and the doctors worried that the side effects would soon outweigh any benefits. Amy and Derrick switched cocktails, dabbled with second generations, and experimented with drugs that had not received the blessing of the FDA. After pushing canister after canister of chemicals into her son, Amy felt that his tiny frame could not possibly hold so many pills. Her final hope was cranial surgery. For almost a year they'd been on a waiting list for the best surgeon in the country. He would open the hood of Aiden's skull and tinker until his brain purred. Amy had imagined the handshake she would give to the surgeon right before he went to work, and the way she would hold Aiden's hand as the drugs withdrew him from consciousness, and how her son would wake up unshakeable.

Despite that hope, Amy worried. It was a constant drip of worry, steady as an I.V. If they didn't heal him quickly, she worried that Aiden would be delayed in his development or permanently impaired. He could lose the ability to speak; he could fail to recognize faces. She worried about Aiden shaking and shaking until he lost consciousness or stopped breathing or his heart gave out. So far, all the episodes had ended within a minute. So far. She tried to think about these scenarios as little as possible, which often led to dwelling on them far too much. Through it all Aiden was an unnaturally good child, so well behaved that when Amy corrected him on minor issues she felt as though she must have misinterpreted the situation.

To help her through the madness, Amy developed a visual technique. She pictured a backdrop of helter-skelter events: hospital beds, splitting pills, her husband departing on weeklong work trips, nighttime tremors, insomnia. Then she superimposed her son's head in the center of all of it. Aiden's face was as round as a children's book character and plain, as if sketched with only a few strokes. He had a purity to his skin that transcended childhood. She found that as she concentrated on his face, the surrounding events would slowly fade, leaving only his wise smile. Only once when she tried this technique—and this was after a several-day stint in the hospital with little sleep—had the visual backfired and Aiden's face vanished, leaving a black oval encircled by the garish, overexposed colors of painful events.

Derrick generally supported her, though they fought over one issue. When Aiden was three, he'd experienced a bad episode at the mall, which ended with security calling paramedics and a rubbernecking crowd, and when they finally reached home Derrick confronted her.

"You were too calm," he'd said.

"Wouldn't you want me to be calm?" she'd asked.

"Too calm," he'd said. "Like you weren't feeling anything. It's because of your father." She'd once told him about a childhood game where her father flicked paper stars at her and she won by not flinching. It sounded cruel but was done in a playful spirit, and as an adult she had not held it against her father. That habit of steeling herself had remained. It was how she and her family had always responded to the furies of life. Derrick had latched onto that story and used it to explain her reactions to things. Sometimes, she thought, it felt like he treated her as the sum of pivotal acts in her life, each act the forefather to a whole set of behavioral grandchildren.

She tried to explain that during the mall incident she wasn't calm, that she was breaking on the inside, but he wouldn't believe her, merely repeating that she'd acted so calm. It was the acting that bothered him, she realized, because he needed someone to give a shape to grief. He wasn't good at it either; he tended to compress his emotions into cryptic cubes. And if he couldn't do it, who was left but her? At that moment, Amy had finally understood why some cultures hired professional mourners to wail over the dead.

Aiden had no play dates, yet their neighbor Nettie Seeger insisted on visiting with her daughter Mabeleine, who was the same age as Aiden. Nettie wore a white dress with black polka dots and a straw hat with floppy folds that took turns obscuring her right or left eye. Amy told Aiden to say hello to Mrs. Seeger.

"Call me Miss Bolton," the neighbor said, giving a high five to Aiden, and added in a lowered voice to Amy, "Going back to the maiden."

In the backyard, they let the children play on the swing and dig in the dirt while they drank lemonade. Over the phone, Amy had told Nettie of Aiden's problem, but it hadn't seemed to register. Nettie said everyone had problems.

"How you doing in the shit-storm of life?" Nettie asked.

The children were close enough to eavesdrop, but they hadn't appeared to hear the profanity. Amy suspected Nettie might have preferred them to hear. "We're fine. We're good. Holding up." She suddenly felt, from the way that Nettie looked at her, that she had a crumb left on her cheeks from lunch, and she brushed at her face to clean it.

"And you and Derrick?" Nettie asked.

"Aiden occupies most of the time. The medicine, the doctor's appointments, everything. The next step is surgery. It has a great success rate."

"It's not only the ones that ditch you that you have to worry about," Nettie said. "Worry about the ones that mentally check out or go on special trips too often."

It took Amy a moment to realize her neighbor was speaking of Derrick, not Aiden. She had pictured Aiden walking down the middle of the street away from the house, clutching an action figure to his chest, never to return. Derrick had arrived in her life as suddenly as a traffic accident, right when she had finally resigned herself to staying single and childless. He was too good of a man to cheat on her; he had debilitating guilt when he committed even the slightest misdeed. By the time Amy disengaged from her own thoughts, Nettie was halfway through the saga of her relationships, which included a bow-tie bartender followed by a flurry of what she called "ethnic experiments." She'd made the mistake of marriage, which had collapsed under the weight of expectations before their first anniversary. "C'est la vie," she said, but as she flung a hand to dramatize her abandonment of that life, Amy noticed her ring finger retained a pale halo of skin.

As Nettie kept talking, Amy considered how frequently she ended up as the listener in a conversation. She was willing to donate her ear because it was expected of her, but ever since Aiden her concentration was flimsy. Her attention was always halved between her child and the speaker. Instead of hearing words, she could only imagine each forthcoming moment as the moment when an attack began. That was what people misunderstood—they thought an attack was the worst time. But during one, Amy knew exactly what to do: cup his head, cradle his body, speak soothing words.

Adrenaline, the patron drug of emergencies, trampled all lesser instincts. No, the darkest moment was on a sunny day like today, when he had been energetic all morning, identical to any other child. The longer he went without incident, the more tension knotted at the base of her neck.

Mabeleine had formed a toy cartel. Every toy Aiden touched, Mabeleine seized. Aiden found one last toy under a bush and instead of keeping it for himself, offered it to Mabeleine, who added it to her hoard. Then he sat, content, and watched her try to wrap her arms around all the toys. He pointed at a boo-boo on Mabeleine's elbow, and she babbled about it. In one gentle gesture, Aiden cupped her arm with both hands before kissing it. He leaned back, smiling in the generous way of a godfather. Aiden offered her his own wounded elbow but she refused. He didn't insist. Sometimes Amy feared he would corrupt those around him because he was so tolerant of others' bad behavior. Amy also worried that if he had an episode now, he would scar poor Mabeleine. Once, Amy took Aiden to the nearby playground, one padded with a forgiving rubber mat made from recycled tires. This was early in the illness and she had not yet reconciled herself to being a recluse. For a half hour, Aiden had played with the other children and Amy had pretended to be a normal mother. Yet when the fit came and she ran to her child and held him, she looked back to find a row of mothers shielding their children's eyes from the horror of her son.

In mid-afternoon Amy bartered promises of future play dates in exchange for Nettie and Mabeleine's departure. Even though Amy had not particularly enjoyed the afternoon, she knew they would spend time together again. Amy would do it for Nettie's sake, even though Amy would have preferred to avoid bad marriage advice, and she would do it for Aiden's sake, since she would listen to a thousand Netties to gain even a single companion for Aiden.

That night she read *Punch the Frog* to Aiden again. Punch finds Rabbit and inflates his cheeks to balloon them up to the surface. Just as Punch and Rabbit crawl onshore, bedraggled and coughing up pond water, Squirrel and Turtle arrive and assume the worst—that Punch tried to drown Rabbit. A crimson wall fills the page behind their towering figures, while at their feet Punch lies, tangled in strips of pondweeds and muddied by earth tones. Rabbit does not speak while the town animals hurt Punch. Squirrel clubs his back and Turtle bites his legs. After they beat Punch so badly he cannot move, they throw him down a deep hole.

Aiden wouldn't let her finish the story that night. He insisted they stop at the hole with the somersaulting Punch disappearing into it. He stared at it happily and she stared at him to avoid it. "Punch is the perfect animal," he said in awe. When Amy said he had to go to bed, he replaced the book on the shelf and promised to fall asleep quickly. His good behavior sometimes unnerved her. When she felt depressed, she wanted to tell him to scribble on the walls and dump cereal on the floor, because even if he didn't have health in common with other children, at least he could misbehave like them.

"Mommy," he said as she turned off the light. "I'm sorry for shaking so much."

She rushed over and hugged him in the dark. "It's not your fault, honey."

"I'm sorry, Mommy. I'm sorry."

She knelt next to the bed and held his hand and told him again and again in a low murmur that it wasn't his fault, until he finally fell asleep.

She found Derrick watching a television movie, the light strobing over the dark living room. He was slumped so deeply into the couch that he appeared sewn into the fabric. She wanted to share with him what Aiden had just said, but she didn't think Derrick wanted to hear it.

"The neighbor came over today," Amy said during a commercial. "And Aiden didn't even have an episode."

"You remember that I'm going to San Francisco for work tomorrow, right?"

"You're leaving me? Why didn't you tell me?"

He insisted that he had, citing time and place, but she didn't remember and suspected he had only meant to tell her. Even if he had spoken it, he had a tendency to cloak the information inside a long speech about a different topic so that it was lost in the folds.

"The seizures are stronger," she said, just as the television blared a fast food commercial and obscured her words.

"It's for three days," Derrick said. "Just the annual checkup of several fields."

She had never seen him doing fieldwork. She imagined him with a clipboard and a hardhat, dwarfed by a field of metallic chickens pecking at the ground. He didn't have an assistant and there were few women in the industry, but she imagined a younger woman at his side, wearing yellow rain boots and a hardhat cocked to the side, who got to spend all day with her husband. For the inspection, he would stop the bobbing chicken head and lean far over the mouth of the well. He would study its every surface and smell, would sound out the depths and fiddle with instruments, then check boxes on his clipboard. Several times she had imagined him losing his footing and falling in, the sides rattling as he hit them on the way down.

"We have Aiden's first appointment with the surgeon on Friday," she said. It was usually the time she could count on his presence, the three of them in a hospital huddle.

"Ask lots of questions," he said. "This is going to work."

"I know it will work," she said. "But I need you there to hear all the surgery details."

He shrugged his excuse. She already knew what he would have said: they had to pay for the hospitals and medicines somehow. That was his role. And he trusted her to absorb all the information; he said he could always trust her to be levelheaded, even though he usually pointed out that trait as though it concealed a deeper flaw.

The morning that Derrick left, she woke before him and made him breakfast. When he rose earlier than he'd said he would, she wondered if he had planned on slipping out unnoticed.

In the kitchen, they leaned on counters and ate oatmeal with cinnamon and bananas. She wanted him to hug and kiss her goodbye but didn't want to prompt him.

"Are you sad that I'm leaving?" he asked.

At first she thought it was a stupid question. But then she heard the accusation—he couldn't tell because she wasn't showing him—and silenced her retort. She didn't want to fight before he headed to a string of lonely hotels. Instead, she slumped her shoulders, stuck out her lower lip and ran her index finger from the corner of her eye down her cheek.

He smiled ruefully. He pretended to turn a crank and hold a hardhat with overdone seriousness. Then he stepped to the right before waving at those activities and exaggerating a shrug.

They could keep going, she thought. They would abolish language and only use signals. It would be their secret code and they would perfect the meanings. They would find the symbols to erode the barriers between them.

But Derrick performed the all-too-everyday movement of setting his bowl in the sink. "Make sure to discipline Aiden," he said. "He's not nearly as holy as you want to believe he is."

He was wrong but she refused to argue. At the door he half turned and half raised his hand in a gesture fit for a colleague's farewell, and she realized that if only she had woken Aiden, and he had stood between them in his pajamas, rubbing crusts from his eyes, Derrick would have turned and embraced her, embraced them. Aiden would have clutched at the fabric around their knees and looked up at the sight of his parents kissing, like two lips of an oyster closing around him, and perhaps years later would remember that image and believe in their love.

Instead, Derrick opened the half-closed gate and disappeared around the corner.

Aiden acted even better once his father had left, as if assuming the mantle of man of the house. The morning after, Amy spied on him from the door as he maneuvered around her bed. As he hummed a tune, he tugged the comforter up to the pillows and tucked the sheets under the mattress. With a heave he threw one leg up onto the mattress, the rest of his body following it. He hit the pillows with ineffectual punches likely meant to fluff them up. He smoothed the wrinkles made by his knees and feet, turning to fix what his knees and feet had messed up, turning again. She didn't care that his shoes left dirt all over the bed.

Aiden saw her. "Mrs. Mommy," he said.

Amy stepped into the room. "Mrs.? Where's this Mrs. coming from?"

"Thank you."

"For what?"

"Thank you for not dying." He leaned in and grabbed the soft flesh of her midsection, the holdover baby flab she'd been unable to vanquish.

"I'm not going to die, sweetheart."

"And thank you for Daddy."

She wrapped up his skinny body and was reminded that she needed to hug him more when he wasn't shaking. His arms around her felt righteous. It would have been a proper moment to cry. And she even felt like crying, but tears wouldn't come.

"Ready to go to the doctor's?" she asked.

The vast parking structure made her feel unimportant, as though Aiden's illness was only driftwood in the sea of sickness. Despite the size, she struggled to find a parking spot.

Inside the hospital the doctor greeted them and crouched to meet Aiden. Amy saw the signs in Aiden's elbows first, a wobble that radiated down and polioed his knees, and the doctor caught him before he hit the ground. Amy witnessed the doctor's genuine sorrow as Aiden convulsed in his arms and she felt jealous of a sorrow so easily and plainly expressed. She knelt beside her son and stroked his hair, but Aiden shook for a long time, longer than he'd ever shaken before, and Amy feared this would be the one, the one where he did not stop shaking. But he finally stopped. After a round of hugs and comforting, Aiden, still crying, hit the nurse who took him away, while Amy sat down at a broad desk. The doctor, who was attractive in an exotic way, had recovered from the incident and projected confidence.

"He's not a good candidate for surgery," the doctor said. The rest of the words were lost on her. She focused on the colored-coded books on the shelf behind him, a testament to the wisdom that could not help her.

"All those books and all these brains and there's nothing else we can do?" she said.

The doctor showed his empty hands to her, as if to prove he had nothing left. "You can wait," he said. "Often they grow out of it."

"When? Why? How?"

"For some children it just stops. Growing bodies, growing brains, things change."

The light from the window caught the doctor's face at a horrid slant, caving in his cheekbones and darkening his eyes sockets. Amy felt repulsed at his sudden ugliness. She'd always believed Aiden's misery would vanish if she could only outlast it, but she now felt all her patience collapsing. On their way out, Aiden kept tripping and she realized she was walking too quickly, almost dragging him by the hand. She slowed but tapped her fingers against her purse. Her car had hid itself in one of the nondescript corners of the structure. She wandered across the lot pushing the key fob without any response, until finally she discovered it on a lower level.

Derrick called before dinner. He always called. Once a day, so regularly it felt like a quota. She yearned for his voice but felt conflicted about answering the phone. No matter his location, every call seemed to push him further away. By the fifth or sixth phone call into a journey, she felt he'd been exiled to some distant, frozen tundra. They talked about Aiden in their usual shorthand, and she kept her voice high, in the falsetto of hope.

"How many?" he asked.

"Five," she said. "A terrible one in the doctor's arms."

"And the doctor said?"

"The surgery won't work," she said.

"What? They said? Why wouldn't?"

She inhaled deeply. "It'll be fine. They'll find something. It'll work out." She spoke quickly and recognized her false poise.

"Maybe they'll come out with new drugs," Derrick said.

She stayed quiet long enough to make him worry. She craved his worry.

"Are you okay?" Derrick asked, then checked himself and answered his own question. "You'll be okay." It sounded more like a command.

"Are *you* okay?" she said.

"Work's going fine."

"I mean about Aiden."

"Of course, you're right. Something will work out."

She couldn't admire his forced optimism. He had cried at their wedding, that much she remembered. And he never seemed to have problems expressing himself during their brief dating relationship. It wasn't until after Aiden started shaking that Derrick walled himself off with the brick and mortar of what he called self-control. He forced all his limbs to keep animated but there was nothing left inside. She'd seen a similar tendency at one of his work parties—a co-worker had slighted him in an off-handed fashion, joking that Derrick couldn't find a hardhat small enough for his head, and while Derrick initially acted good naturedly, he didn't smile for the rest of the evening. He didn't frown either. There wasn't any mystery about his expression, only the sense that whatever he did feel had retreated several steps back from his skin, into some deep cavity perhaps not even he could access.

A shuffling of papers came over the phone, his sound-track of impatience, and she reluctantly tendered her goodbye.

On the third day of Derrick's absence, Aiden had a terrible morning with seven episodes, one of which reinjured his elbow, before Amy lured him into an early afternoon nap. In the kitchen, a low whir came through the open window from the hummingbirds visiting the sugar-water feeder. Dust settled on the furniture and dressers, each particle piling on audibly. Her hands felt unnaturally empty. She went to the closet to fetch cleaning supplies but the corner of her easel, protruding from beneath other junk that had not been touched for ages, reproached her with all the paintings that had not made it to canvas. In the end, she neither cleaned nor painted. She felt reckless, afraid of what she might do.

Last night Aiden had called to her: "Pick up and read. Pick up and read!" She had read the book again to Aiden, for the hundredth time, and the repetition had not dulled its haunting effect. For the last six pages of the book, Punch is in the hole where the others tossed him. The pages are uniformly black, even the margins, save for a shear of light across Punch's face. Beside him are bits of carrots and celery, thrown to him, presumably, by Rabbit. He faces the reader, with faint light glinting off a bruised eye, and says that the life of Rabbit was worth his beating and imprisonment. He says that even the innocent are punished and he will happily sacrifice for others. He says he will give and give of himself and he will never run out. On the last page, shown from a height beyond the eagles, a dragonfly hovers over the pond and a fish beneath it, and reeds sway next to a pyramid of rocks. At the center of the page is that black hole, but from that hole comes a series of musical notes, as if in Punch the Frog's near future there will be joyful song. When she finished reading the book, Aiden turned to her with the gravity of an adult and said, "She did it for me." And he pressed his scabbed elbow to Punch's mouth and made a kissing sound. "Punch is now a she?" she'd said to him, quite surprised. But he didn't explain. He just looked at her as though surprised she didn't already know.

Amy checked on Aiden to make sure he was asleep before leaving the house through the kitchen and walking into the cleft of light between the backyard trees. The sun beat down thuggishly and a breeze glided down the San Gabriel Mountains, orienting the leaves in uniform directions. Distant traffic hummed. She didn't realize what was happening until her vision blurred and her hands lost their power. She deflated, first going to her knees before reaching her stomach. Scrub grass grated against her hip; a weed's cowlick battered her shin. She could taste dirt. Her whole body shook with great, wracking sobs. Against the screen of her closed eyelids, a series of threatening black spots appeared, similar to the ones at the edge of her vision when she stood up too fast. It was all gone, gone; she had nothing left to give. She had emptied herself yet the universe greedily demanded more. She felt ready to give up, yet what that entailed frightened her so much she refused to imagine specific plans. Her tears mixed with the dirt and left a paste of mud on her cheeks.

"Mommy!" The tremors of little feet pounded over the dirt. "Mommy, Mommy, Mommy!"

She willed herself up to a sitting position and brushed her face and hair clean. Aiden raced toward her, stumbling in his haste. At first she worried that he'd seen her on the ground and become anxious that he'd passed his sickness on to her, but his expression was one of rapture.

"Mommy, I'm healed!"

For a swift moment she believed it was true. An airbag of hope inflated her chest. A single number pounded through her brain: zero, zero, zero, zero. But when Aiden skidded at her feet and presented his elbow, the elbow wounded from his falls, her fantasies lurched to a stop. Her disappointment must have shown because he pushed the elbow closer to her, as if she hadn't seen it correctly. This time she noticed that his scratch and the scab had indeed disappeared, as if he'd received a graft of new skin.

"See?" he said, using a finger to mark his insistence. She knew what he needed, and she knew just what to do.

"You're beautiful and healthy," she said, smiling madly, and she held him so tightly he grunted. As the sun brightened around them, turning the yard into a field of sequins, she held her hope tightly and waited.

To Will One Thing

On the night Will felt the floating sensation, he attended a performance of the Ugandan Boys Choir. The boys were trash scavengers, rescued by a Good Samaritan and taught to harmonize, who performed every night across California to raise donations and recruit volunteers for the Kampala orphanage. Will attended by himself, since Regina was at the baby shower for a college friend's third child. This was the friend who'd called Regina, offhandedly and without malice, a ringless fiancée, by which she meant a woman certain to marry but lacking the diamond. Regina had grieved over the term for weeks.

The Ugandan Boys sang in the church for two hours. Terraced upon metallic risers, they elongated their jaws. On one song, the boys left the stage to pass donation baskets, and the volume and balance fluidly shifted as the voices swung close and away. The music seized Will. It offered odd time signatures, syncopated rhythms, contrapuntal notes. Despite his usual formality inside sacred walls, he found himself tapping his foot and nodding in tempo. Instead of his normal instinct to pin down feelings with philosophical thoughts, he wanted to run through fields and not grow weary. He wanted to swim and not grow tired. He wanted this soundtrack to animate his life.

Will closed his eyes. The melodies became flags, waving to the beat. The notes danced and died and regenerated. Then his chair seemed to exhale him, and the floor released his feet. The pressure on his buttocks eased. He hovered, feeling weightless as a bubble. His skin felt permeable, with no membrane between air and flesh. The sensation continued until the precise moment when—as if synchronized—the last note terminated. Then his body settled, tethered again. Applause erupted around him. He gripped the chair, breath drumming in his ears. He felt like he'd been attacked. He turned to the woman behind him and asked her if she saw it. "Yes, they're great," the woman said, nodding towards the choir, still clapping. Everyone stood in an ovation. No one paid him any attention. As the audience flooded the front to talk to the boys, he fled through the double doors, feeling pursued.

He told Regina the following day, when they were on the couch with her dead aunt's quilt. Though he preferred to rest in her room, Regina judged privacy a stumbling block to purity. He read. She knitted. Her long hair kept interfering with her needles. It'd grown past her waist, requiring the choke points of several bands. He often found Rapunzel-length strands in his car.

"Six months?" she said. "Uganda?"

"I didn't say I was going," he said. "They just offered the opportunity." He would miss her too much to go. Last summer, when he'd flown to a weeklong car convention in Denver, he called her twice a day. And there was no question of her accompanying him—their families would raise an outcry if they traveled together unmarried. They hadn't even kissed. Influenced by the popular books in home-school circles, she'd made a promise—she didn't swear, she refused to swear—not to kiss anyone but her husband. He respected her belief because he knew it would hurt her deeply to break that promise.

She'd stopped clicking her needles, a sound so metronomic he found himself adjusting his breath to match its pace. "Getting married is an adventure, too," she said.

"And I want that," he said. After all, he'd filled his quotient of adventure on two mission trips in his college years, to Indonesia and Samoa. She was living her adventure now, swarmed by toddlers at the day care. Once, he'd surprised her at work with flowers, and discovered her bracing bottle-sucking girls off both hips, while using a knee to push a boy on the swing who screamed, "Higher! Higher!" She was beaming.

"You do this," she said. "Remember dog breeding in Kentucky? Remember that Iranian underground-church plan?"

"You're right," he said. "It was silly to even bring it up."

"It was," she said.

When he first met Regina, at a brother- and sister-wing bowling night, she'd rolled a strike and curtsied. He'd stored that clip in his head, replaying it often. It was such a graceful act—the pinch of dress between index and thumb, the right foot bent behind, the chin dipped. She seemed a quaint maid transplanted from a bygone time. A month passed before he'd started courting her. She preferred that term to dating.

She used her thumb to rotate her purity ring. "Do you love me more than anything?"

"No," he said.

Her head jerked. "Well, not more than God, of course," she added hastily.

"Right," he said. But he knew what she needed and gave it to her: he said that he loved her, that there was no one else, that she was beautiful.

She kneeled and lowered her head to the coffee table, so all he could see was the part in her blonde hair that exposed a vulnerable line of her scalp. He said her first name: once loudly, once quietly. He said her full name—Regina Sarah Olsen—but not even that unlocked her. Finally, she lifted her head. "If you really wanted to go, you could go," she said. The words rang hollow.

"I wasn't really considering it."

"Well," she said. "I just wouldn't want to hold you back." It sounded straight from a cue card. Still, the possibility resonated in his chest, as if all his organs were tuned to the pitch of her permission.

She offered gifts. Usually she didn't gift him except on birthdays and Christmas, but now she sprung them at random. At her apartment one night, he found her in an apron dusted with flour, both hands behind her back. She whipped out a gift-wrapped object, and he unwrapped it to find a book about the Icelandic chess match between Bobby Fisher and Boris Spassky during the Cold War. He hugged thanks. Afterwards, she fed him hot scones, tipping her fingers up at the end to help him eat each bite. He made Neanderthal chomping sounds and she squealed when he pretended to bite her fingers. When he said he didn't want more, she insisted. She made engine noises and flew flight patterns until he relented.

One night, after working until nine, he found a pastel envelope fluttering under the gums of his windshield wipers. A card bearing her florid handwriting, the large cursive loops on the l's and f's, which, according to a manual on handwriting psychology he'd read, indicated a generous ego. In the card she flung a largesse of compliments, not the cheap trinkets that any stranger could trot out, but the genuine coin. It was one of her best traits, this way she had of loving him. He read it twice.

He drove to the bookstore with the intention of buying her a book. During a recent facelift, the store had shuffled their sections and he couldn't find the cookbooks. Instead, he found himself on a long aisle with neon-colored spines. Just as he reached the end, a book cart wheeled up, blockading him. He backtracked, noticing the spines belonged to travel guides. He didn't want to linger, but glanced over the titles. At eye level, out of alphabetical order, were three yellow Ugandan guidebooks. Why three? He would have guessed the store only carried the regional book. He leafed through, feeling guilty. Reading the introductory notes, he realized he knew nothing of Uganda—their language, their currency, their politics. All his knowledge came from the tired Western views of the continent, as if Africa were a homogenous blotch on the globe. He bought the guidebook, just to look at the pictures. Nothing more. Afterwards, he realized he'd forgotten to buy the cookbook, and when he met Regina and friends for board game night, he only said that he'd been browsing.

Will and Regina attended a wedding in a spacious backyard. Regina and the bride had homeschooled together for years, and Regina relayed to him multiple times the story of the bride and groom meeting, betrothing, and marrying within eight months. Paper lanterns swung from strings, apple cider filled the flutes, an aging Christian singer crooned from the stereo. Regina was not unhappy. Although there was no formal dancing, she swung the tuxedoed arms of her five-year-old brother. Will sat at the pink-creped table and watched the dignity of the bride and pent-up anticipation of the groom, the children chasing one another with party favors clutched in chubby hands. He knew these people. These were his people. They would keep attending church, keep elevating God, keep their marriage vows, keep raising their children in the ways they should go. Tragedies would be chalked up to the divine plan, and suffering embraced as a purifying force. Nothing truly unpredictable would happen: Butler would gain weight, Alison's grandparents would tour the country in their motor home, the twins would win tennis tournaments. He could see five years, ten years, and knew that nothing would rupture their course. This, this. He wanted only this. With this he could be happy.

"I have something to confess," Will told her one sunny day, while they were at bat against a Valencia church. This wasn't the place; he could feel how wrong it was. Sports warped the delicate bonds between males and females. A foul ball soared, outfielders bobbing heads to spot it and avoid their teammates. She didn't wait for the pop fly resolution, just turned to him. She looked good in the loose jeans, dusted red from the last inning. Usually he only saw her in dresses. "I emailed the orphanage," he said. The phrase resounded in the space between them. He felt like he'd hit her.

"That's nice," she said, turning away. Then she gripped the dugout railing and yelled at the new batter: "C'mon, Lacey! Sock it!" He leaned back and waited for her to process and turn, angrily, but she didn't. Normally, she let him make the hefty decisions, like whether to drive together to her Uncle's house in San Francisco. She would act as though she didn't care, although sometimes she did. Now, even though she couldn't tell a shortstop from a catcher, she kept her focus on the game: the bark of the bat, the soar of the ball into the low sky, the outfielders scrambling to bottom it. She cheered and pumped a fist.

But in a way, he was relieved that she hadn't pressed him. If she had, he would have admitted he didn't want to email the orphanage. That he didn't want to go at all. It was an email in a moment of thoughtlessness, about which he felt shameful, as if he'd gone to the wrong website and seen something he shouldn't.

◆ ◆ ◆

In the shed at his parent's house, his father soldered a scepter onto a queen. On the shelf, bishops apexed in a bulb and knights brandished swords from winged horses. The blade of the TIG torch seared his vision. His father swung off his hood and asked, "Ready to get whooped?"

They sat on either side of the upended wooden spool. This set was cast in geometric shapes: blocks for pawns, stacked balls for queens, triangles for bishops. His father got two glasses of lemonade, even though Will knew they'd forget to drink it, and secreted a black and white pawn in each fist. Will picked the right fist. White. Just before he moved, his father asked, "Now what's this about Uganda?"

Up to that moment, Will had been deluded enough to believe that Regina hadn't truly heard or didn't care. But she must have deliberately dropped a comment, probably to his mother, which cascaded to his father. His parents wanted a quiver of grandchildren. The delay of several years seemed fruitless. And Regina knew they thought this way.

Will told him about the choir, trying to explain it offhandedly.

"Why would you want to go?" his father said.

"I don't even know," Will said. "I probably don't want to."

"I know why," his father said. "You have a good heart and want to help people."

It sounded like a solid reason, and Will let his father think it was the correct one. His father lived that way, helping people through the part-time work at the church and janitorial work for school, working despite the migraines. It was always about others. His father replied to the opening with the Budapest Gambit and slapped the clock vigorously. He'd played on the circuit with his junior college team but now spent most of his chess time building custom sets. Obscene requests were denied, but he'd built sets of New

York/Los Angeles architecture and Roman emperors holding coins bearing their image.

"So did they get back to you?" his father asked.

"The orphanage? Yes. They gave details." The details were draconian. Four volunteers slept in one small room. Food was austere. It was less of an enticement and more of a warning.

"You shouldn't go," his father said. "You've got too much to lose."

His father traded a bishop for two of Will's pawns and pushed his queenside. Will tried to blockade with a knight. Flies landed on the pieces and Will shooed them away. When Will was five, his mother found him sleeping in a laundry basket with a chessboard and pieces, and his father joked that he'd started playing in the womb. The day after his grandfather died, Will played a marathon session, and after he and Regina fought, he often retreated to an online site for blitz games.

His father advanced a pawn. "She can't wait forever," he said.

"I know," Will said.

His father once built a religious chess set. Christ, Gabriel, disciples versus Satan, demons, possessed. When he told people about it, he asked them to guess which side was white. Then he'd laugh loudly. For some years he showcased the set on his website, but sold it because he didn't like the possibility of black winning. Will liked the set concept—it implied that even the powers and principalities played by reason. And his father agreed, proposing that parishioners should play chess before church services, to usher them into God's mode of thinking.

His father studied the board, elbows on the table. Will didn't think he saw it. The next move Will would sacrifice a bishop. Once he sacrificed the bishop, the rest of the game would be inevitable. His father moved and Will replied. The move made his father inhale. There would be a smothered mate on h8 in seven moves. Every variation was accounted for, every sequence anticipated. The pure inevitability was beautiful. But when his father swung his hands out in frustration, he knocked over a glass of lemonade. It shattered on the concrete and Will felt a shiver against his pinky toe. Blood dewed from a cut. By the time they cleaned up the glass and sanitized the wound, his mother arrived home with groceries, and after they unpacked them, Will had to meet Regina. The game was lost. His father joked that he should injure opponents more often. "Like in chessboxing," he said. He ducked his head and pretended to jab twice.

Will was five years old, on his back. Bees hummed around his head. Oak branches sliced up the sky. Someone had yelled something he hadn't understood. Black clouds formed and dissipated across his vision, and inside these clouds, blurred shapes of men and animals moved, as if seen through a dark glass. When the clouds stopped, the sky kaleidoscoped through the rainbow's spectrum. He tasted colors. Burnt, smoky copper. Floral, breezy gold. Then it all settled and the world righted itself. He started crying. Scruffy approached and licked his face. There was the bang of the screen door; there was the rapid flap of his mother's sandals. She knelt and cupped his head and plied him with questions, and he could only remember playing with his truck, followed by the loud voice and the clouds and the colors. "What loud voice?" she asked. He said his head hurt. He wasn't bleeding. He bore no marks.

One doctor diagnosed it as a strange type of stroke, and prescribed medication. Another doctor argued his body bore the signs of an electrical shock, a magnitude on par with lightning. His mother insisted there were no outlets or

extension cords in the backyard and no clouds in the sky.
Another doctor said nothing had happened, that his brain
needed to discharge energy and he'd experienced powerful
yet illusory sensations. They gave up going to doctors. Their
degree of certainty directly correlated to their degree of
inaccuracy. A few admitted their inability to pin down a
reasonable answer, and told his mother to watch for a
reoccurrence so more data could be gathered. But it hadn't
happened again, not like that, not for years.

In an early draft of his application for the philosophy
program at The Lord's College, Will told that story. It seemed
a seminal moment, even though he'd never been able to
assign it a precise role. Instinctively, he knew it explained
why he wanted to study analytic philosophy, but couldn't
tell how. In a vague way he believed that philosophy could
ward off events like that one, but since philosophers had to
be able to clearly draw from point A to point B, he eventually
cut it, substituting an essay on how he inherited the ideals
of chess from his father.

She kissed him. It was never meant to be that order of
subject and object. He kissed her: that was how he'd always
envisioned it. That order, he thought, was the only way that
she would ever have wanted it. Allow the man to be the
leader. After all, when they first started spending time
together, she wouldn't call him, insisting he should call her.
But here she'd seized initiative.

They'd guided the junior high youth group to Magic
Mountain and ridden the newest coaster. During the
corkscrew at the end, his vision dimmed, as though someone
twisted a knob for the lights. All the light funneled into the
center then faded to black, and even the passengers' screams
decrescendoed. In that tunnel without exit he felt the
terrifying sensation of losing control, and then the corkscrew

straightened out to pull up to the platform and light and sound ebbed back.

They sat on a bench semi-blocked by bushes and she asked whether he was okay. He lied and said yes, forcing a smile. The smile triggered her.

He didn't know how they'd dated for three years and never kissed. No, he knew. Her hirsute father who required an interview before granting permission to date his daughter. The group dates for the first six months, followed by chaperoned ones. Her mother telling the story of how the only person she'd ever kissed was Regina's father. Regina's reluctance to hold hands until a year had passed, and of course her promise to keep her lips virginal. Add to that his fear of himself, of losing control. Of believing passion in their marriage would be lost if he prematurely opened the gate of pleasure.

They spent a half hour on the bench, primly exploring each other's lips. He'd expected to feel untamed. He'd always feared the urges of his loins. But the sensation gave him an odd detachment, a pleasurable distance from which he analyzed the situation. There were two people on a bench. They were kissing. It was a scene he'd watched thousands of times, and even this time he remained more a viewer than a participant. She giggled. She fingered her long braid curled in her lap. He ignored the passersby, then glanced at them with embarrassment. A man carrying a cluster of balloons stopped across the way. As he detached a purple balloon for a girl, a red one wriggled loose and soared, weaving in its ascent.

Her line at the end disappointed him. He would have preferred a romantic mood, unleavened by laughter, but instead, as they moved to find the junior highers, she teased him: "Wouldn't you miss that?" Motives curdled the moment. Instead of the supernova of a long-awaited pleasure, it seemed calculated. He suspected why she said it: earlier in the day, a mob of black children passed by, corralled by two black ladies who alternated between gaiety and reprimands, and he turned to look at the children, feeling nostalgic about an experience he had not yet had. She saw him look and he saw her interpret.

He meant to only peck her when he dropped her off at her apartment, but couldn't resist lingering. On the drive home, he admitted that despite his aversion to her method, it certainly worked. He would miss that, if he were crazy enough to leave. He would miss it terribly.

At that backyard wedding they'd attended, Will had heard Regina's Uncle Roy tell a story about a distant British relative of the Olsen clan. The man had left his wife one day, just walked out the front door and did not come back. Apparently, he moved just a few blocks over and changed his job. He spied on her but never contacted her. There was no mistress. It was a loving marriage. Eventually his wife counted him among the dead. They held a funeral. He spied on the funeral. Once he walked past his wife on the street and his wife did not recognize him. A few months after the funeral, he returned to his own house during the night and settled into bed. In the early morning hours, his wife woke and found a strange man occupying her bed. Nothing about him made her think he might have been her former husband. So she seized a letter opener and stabbed him. When he cried out, she recognized his voice. She called an ambulance and paramedics saved him.

That was where the story ended. The circle broke up to attend to misbehaving children. But Will asked Uncle Roy what happened. Uncle Roy said the couple had gone to therapy, not that it helped. The man was impenetrable. He didn't fight the therapist, he just had nothing inside him that the therapist found helpful. The man didn't know why he had left or why he had come back. He seemed as confused about it as everyone else, except that he knew he'd needed to leave. His wife had gone to see the brownstone where her husband had lived, but someone else had already rented it. Apparently, he'd thrown everything in a dumpster. A clean break. He wanted to pick up life where they'd left off. The story happened twenty years ago, and from that time he'd been a devoted husband.

The next day Will told Regina he hated the story. It made him feel sick.

"Oh, that story's not true," Regina said. "Uncle Roy embellishes all the time."

Will countered that her father and aunts had not questioned the story, but Regina insisted it was made-up. Her head wagged no, as if swinging along a deep groove. Suddenly he knew that whatever its truthfulness, she couldn't accept it. He realized: even if she were the wife of that man, she wouldn't believe the story.

That night insomnia haunted him, despite his usual trick of squeezing the pressure point between thumb and index. He rose and sat at the dining table. His roommate's snores bored through the door. The cabinets and furniture took on new contours, reshaped by generous shadows and stingy light. He started a list. Lists organized the world, offering neat parameters and channels. On one side, Negative: Career, parents, money, physical love, and above all, Regina. His pen lingered over the Positive side without committing to the page. Finally, in a bid to put a word down, he wrote, "Called?" Then he jammed the list in the trash beneath the chicken carcass and returned to his bed where he lay, sleepless, watching moonlight drift across the floor from the fulcrum of the blinds. He worried about experiencing one of his moments, but felt nothing.

◆ ◆ ◆

He and Regina walked near his apartment, following a meandering path through the tree-canopied canyon. It was on the outskirts of the city, full of low ranch houses splayed out on multiple-acre plots. The imprints of horse hooves appeared fossilized in the ground. Even though it was January, an autumnal palette of leaves clung to the trees.

They talked of teaching a Sunday school lesson about Abraham and Isaac and of visiting Santa Barbara with her parents and seven siblings. They talked of the new program that automatically censored foul language from movies. He had the feeling she was avoiding any mention of Uganda, so he hinted at the topic by saying that his boss promised a chance at promotion if he didn't hightail it to a foreign country.

She shrank into herself, as though storing up energy before a launch. "I think I know why you feel compelled to go," she said. She threw her shoulders back the way she did before every spiel. Then she launched into his record of service in college: missionary, soup-server, poverty minister, worship leader, camp counselor. A poster child of self-sacrifice. "And what do you do now?" she said. "Now you rent cars. Now you make money. Now you focus only on yourself and me. It's no wonder that you feel like you need to give a little again." She seemed satisfied by this explanation, as if hoping the sense of it would overcome his urges.

The logic was inescapable. She'd put words to something he'd once imagined: himself in that Greek myth where the protagonist stares at his reflection until he dies. Except in his case, there wasn't one reflection but hundreds. Hundreds of mirrors surrounding him, all showing himself to himself, and it was horrifying. But that vision came only in a moment of doubt. He had created ways to give of himself, to her and to his community, even though not at the same rate. Of course he wanted to give more, but that wouldn't justify a continental leap. "That's not bad," he admitted. "But I think it's beyond that."

"Beyond it to what?"

Will thought of a man playing a flute through the streets, and those who streamed out to follow him. He thought of images flashed so quickly that the naked eye couldn't detect them. He thought of the trigger words used by hypnotists to set their subjects in motion. "To listening?" he said.

They walked on. He noted every item in their path, as if later he could revisit the order and quilt a patchwork of meaning. Hull of a snail, a fake mustache, an atlas page. He didn't know how the conversation turned dark. Her tears arrived without warning. She began complaining that he was keeping her emotionally hostage. "Make a decision," she said. "Tell me you won't leave me."

"Every day I make the decision to stay," he said.

"That means any day you could go."

He pictured himself walking out of her apartment and never going back. The idea scared him more than any nightmare. He doubted he had that willpower. He didn't want that willpower. Her eyes scanned his face, reading the lines of his cheeks, his mouth, the ridge between eyebrows. She must have disliked what she saw.

"I didn't want to show you this, but I will," she said.

They drove back to her apartment and she set up the laptop. A video clip with yesterday's date. The BBC's accents dignified even the most tragic events. It showed men in tattered jerseys waving rifles from the back of trucks. The ticker tape read "January Massacre." The voiceover related the political troubles in Kenya, and the map flashed the long border with Uganda. Key phrases surfaced: fleeing refugees, destabilized government, dominoing violence. The images veered from skinny men in oversized T-shirts shooting weapons to clusters of men pumping fists in the air. The segment ended on a shot of a muddy pond, with lumpy bags stacked on the shore. Then he realized. Those were not bags. Those were not bags.

"You hadn't heard," she said.

He imagined bullets strafing over his head or militants holding him for ransom. During college, his friend's mission trip to India had been canceled because of a nuclear standoff between India and Pakistan, and everyone understood: you couldn't visit the volatile regions.

"Sorry," she said. Her eyes looked daubed with blush. "I'd hoped not to show you."

"No, thanks. I—"

"Right," she said. "You shouldn't."

"Of course not. I can't."

She replayed the video without sound. The jump cuts flashed rhythmically. The colors seemed brighter, the action quicker. Men's mouths formed O's of silent exaltation. Will turned away at the end, but Regina didn't. She stared as the screen's glow brightened over her face, her own mouth slowly expanding into an oval. Then she closed the laptop screen and the room fell dark.

He drove back to his apartment so slowly that two cars honked at him. There did not seem to be a road; he drove mechanically, by memory. The lights of opposing vehicles refracted as if through prisms. When he stared at them without focusing, the gyre of light widened until it diffused and his sight refocused on the narrow beams. There must have been a parking space; there must have been a walk to the door.

Inside his apartment, he stood at his bedroom window. He lived with his roommate on the third floor, overlooking the park at the base of the loamy hills where he'd once picnicked with Regina. A memorial service consecrated the park—the bobbing candles looked like a revolving galaxy. He blocked out the view and leaned his head against the window. It cooled a strip on his forehead. All the distant sounds of a neighbor revving a car and his roommate's television drained away. Each breath expanded and deflated his entire frame, the air reaching even his thighs, his head, until even his breath vanished, and he felt motionless, suspended in a vat of fluid. His head grew light, as though the blood flushed from his brain and coalesced in his chest. Then he sensed, behind eyelids, the entire room swell, objects blooming so close that he felt shrunk by their magnitude, and the shifting sizes disoriented him. His ears hurt; his equilibrium swam. It tilted him, made him drift. This time, he didn't fight it. He let the objects press against him, overwhelm him. He sensed his own body enlarging to match their dilated size and was not afraid.

When he finally opened his eyes, he felt it. A breaker had flipped, and all of the uncertainty had settled and flattened. This he realized: all the reasons were stacked against his going, and he would still do it. He was meant to fling himself into a future he could not read. He went down to the computer, placed in the public space of the living room to encourage moral internet habits. From the kitchen came the sounds of his roommate, the shuffle of socks and clack of dishware. Although Will knew precisely what airline, what time, what website, he still ran one last check, to confirm someone hadn't scaled the price down. He had a distressing vision that the airline had swooned out of business or that rising oil had spiked the ticket price, but nothing had changed.

When he pressed the button to buy the plane ticket, he remembered a cliff in Mexico, at the lip of the frothy sea.

After his short-term team had finished building houses, they'd gone to the Caribbean coast and taken turns jumping from this cliff. It wasn't too high, only about twenty feet, but when he was on top, it looked more like forty. The waves came in, the waves left. A sliding hue of dark blue, light blue, and grainy beige. If he didn't time the leap right, he'd hit rock. He measured the rhythms and coaxed his heartbeat into preparing his legs. Then the moment of ditching the ground, of sailing out and over. His throat tightening up. Arms flailing. Legs flexed from the force of the jump. The bubbling up of vertigo, the uplift of a freefall armed with only timing and hope. It was a feeling he'd missed.

Back in his bedroom, gripping a printout of the confirmation number, he eyed his backpack and closet, knowing it was too soon to pack but already cataloguing the list of supplies. A chamois instead of a towel. Pure DEET instead of the diluted version because it took less space. Pants that zipped off to make shorts. He tasted tears before he realized he was crying. He wiped them from his smiling lips and left them on his cheeks. Though he hoped she would forgive him, he felt that she would not. In the center of the room, surrounded by the debris that would soon be separated into staying and going, he held out his hands, palms up, clenching and releasing, clenching and releasing. It felt good. He kept repeating the motion, imagining spheres rising from his opening palms to drift along the ceiling, each departing one reducing his weight until he felt he might float. Then he thought he heard, perhaps from the kitchen or from even farther, someone say his name.

In the Dark Heart of the Fojas

In late afternoon the humidity turned from soup to gel, and wearing a fifty-pound backpack didn't help. Vines draped between trees as if hoping to clothesline us and the silhouettes of monkeys skittered between distant branches. My brother led the way without ever looking behind him, as if it wouldn't be a problem if he lost me. Not that it surprised me. He'd been trying to lose me his entire life. He only brought me on this trip as a last option, because everyone else he knew was tied to mortgages and children, and I had only come because of a mistaken belief that it would earn me a little respect. We navigated between two hills because my brother suspected the missionaries would have taken the easiest route, then stopped to make camp.

"How are your feet?" Kyle asked. In the week before we left, he kept repeating that our feet were the most important body part to safeguard.

"The blisters popped," I said. Yesterday we'd forded a stream and I hadn't changed to dry socks. "How are the bites?"

He examined the two marks on his shoulder, twin pools of pus stagnating beneath red caps. We didn't know what had bitten him. "Same."

They didn't look the same. They looked much worse, swollen and hardened. We'd already applied our first aid supplies, mostly ointments and bandages, which had done nothing. It worried me. Out here in the Fojas, so isolated you could only helicopter in, so mountainous that satellite phones couldn't vault the terrain, death was a real possibility. Our missionaries were the third group in modern history to come. I shouldn't say "our" missionaries, because my brother and I believed nothing that they did. We were only here to rescue them from themselves.

I fired up the Sterno and he dug freeze-dried beef stroganoff from his backpack. Our water filter had broken the first day, so we had to purify the stream water with iodine, which made our water taste metallic. We sat on our backpacks because Kyle insisted logs could camouflage scorpions or ants, and we ate until the last smears disappeared from the pouches.

The world darkened and slid into the sounds of night. Eyes glowed from a faraway tree. Insects fluttered against my cheek and neck. I hated night.

"One more day before we start backtracking," I said. "Five days in, five days out."

"We can't go back without them," he said. "We can't."

We would if we didn't find any clues soon. I wasn't about to die trying to save some idiot missionaries, but my brother wielded the compass and these missionaries were his wife Marie's brothers. If he wasn't so stubborn, he wouldn't have kept flogging his real estate business after its death, and we would be turning back instead of playing rainforest roulette with our lives.

We erected the tent and settled back on our bags. The night burst with sound. Monkeys squeezed in their last shrieks, cicadas sawed away, and the underbrush rustled with ambitious critters. Every tissue of my body ached with exhaustion. Tomorrow we'd repeat today, failing to find any trace of human presence as we trudged through this maze of plants, trying to save the people who'd come to save others.

The next day, hiking again, primeval mud slurped at our boots. Yellow and red frogs were underfoot, leaping out of the way just in time. I did double takes on the fanned-out, serrated leaves that looked like the right leaf, but thankfully my brother didn't notice. It had been over a week since my last toke, and I missed it. My brother checked the compass again and maintained his course. Over the past few days I'd started to doubt his skill with directions. Sometimes he would hold the compass at a slight angle instead of flat, and shake it as if forcing the needle to show him what he wanted to see.

A white possum, with rheumy eyes and foamy mouth, crossed our path, sniffed blindly and without interest, and doddered off. If Kyle's brothers-in-law had survived, they'd probably resorted to eating animals like that, roasting them on a spit until the sockets charred. Or they'd found natives to convert and decided to live with them. Not that anyone knew for sure that natives existed. Before we flew here there had been some speculation over whether we'd encounter cannibals—they did exist, in these backwoods of the world—but that seemed so fantastical, like a bad television show. If the missionaries were dead, it was probably less sensational, like they'd eaten the wrong root or mushroom.

"You shouted again last night," I told my brother as we hiked.

He didn't turn. "Did I? I'm sorry."

"Something about it not working. And then you eased back to sleep." I didn't mention he shouted his wife Marie's name.

My brother looked at the compass and shook it. "It's working."

He was hiking too fast, without paying attention, which made him miss the blotch of black just off our course, and when I pushed through a veil of ferns I discovered what we had been looking for. The rain couldn't disguise the evidence—a horseshoe of stones ringed a pile of soot. This was it. But just before shouting to my brother, I hesitated. On this, the last day before we should turn around, we didn't need to discover evidence. It would be hard enough already to convince him to go back. I did want to save James and John, but I wanted my own life more. Just as I began to back away, my brother shouted my name and found me.

He danced and sang an upbeat tune with made-up words. He only stopped singing to make grand claims about how he knew we were close, how he knew we were going the right direction. He was not a dancer or a singer, and even though we were probably hundreds of kilometers from other human beings, I was embarrassed on his behalf.

We split to search the surrounding area for more clues. I found leaves shaped like fish spines and fleur-de-lis and taper candles, a mushroom village with striped caps, and a bird performing a mating ritual by flaring his comb into a mohawk. At the base of larger trees, trunks split into fins, like missiles ready for launch. No more clues, though. Just the same chlorophyll-choked rainforest, offering so much of a single color my eyes felt tinted green.

When I returned to the ashes, Kyle was already back. He knelt over his bag, his hands clasped together, eyes closed and mouth moving.

"Don't do that," I said, surprised because he'd never pledged that allegiance and it stank of desperation.

"Don't do what?" he said, swiveling. He'd spun so quickly I knew I must have been wrong. Then he seemed to realize what I'd concluded from his body. "No, of course I wasn't—" I knew what he meant and felt apologetic. Likely he'd only been muttering mottos to himself while tightening up his bag. Even though he'd married into a religious family, neither of us had grown up believing in anything but ourselves.

We stood around the ashes while he studied the ground, even though the rain over the last month guaranteed no marks would remain. But Kyle grew his confidence in a greenhouse so it wouldn't be harmed by the weather of the real world. "They went this way," he said, pointing in a random direction.

That night we lay on top of our sleeping bags listening to the traffic and courtship of animals. We had hiked for another four hours, until reaching a flat stretch where the twilight failed to penetrate the canopy. He hadn't mentioned it, but I'd seen his festering shoulder when he'd changed shirts. It had shifted into the type of mottled color that doesn't heal on its own.

"I keep worrying that I've forgotten to pay taxes or get building permits," Kyle said.

In the two weeks we'd spent together, preparing and hiking, it was the first time he'd mentioned work to me, and he said it in a reverent tone. He hadn't even told me the development company he'd spearheaded had collapsed in the housing crash—I'd learned that from our mother. The company died six months ago, but I'd only found out last month, right about the time his in-laws mobilized to call the Red Cross, the American embassy in Jakarta, and the Indonesian government, to discover that the disappearance of James and John would be investigated by no one. Given that his father-in-law was wheelchair-bound, the duty fell to unemployed Kyle. We didn't even have enough money or time to hire a guide, not that anyone knew this godforsaken patch of the world.

I rolled on my side to face him. "Your next job shouldn't keep you up at night."

"I wouldn't want a job that didn't keep me up at night."

A faint glow buzzed against the tent wall, like a firefly searching for an opening. "The kind of job I like? Remembering what beers and shots to pour. Makes life easy, man."

My brother made a derogatory whoosh. "That's only because you're still—" He pinched his index and thumb, pressed them to his lips and sucked.

"C'mon, don't go there."

"Got you into trouble in high school, but you didn't learn your lesson."

Just because I'd been high both times I got girls pregnant in high school, somehow, in his mind, pot was tied to embarrassments and abortions. "What lesson was I supposed to learn? I wore a condom both times. The boys just kept getting past the goalie."

"How unlucky," my brother said, his voice serrated.

I sweated against the nylon casing of the sleeping bag. We'd only used the bags as padding, since even at night the rainforest felt like a sauna. "When are you and Marie finally going to get pregnant?" I asked.

The local noise paused. Without the chattering of animals, I could hear the thick presence of the leaves around us. The tent tightened until I felt uncomfortably close to him.

"I just need to bring back her brothers," he said. "That's what I'm going to give her."

The animals resumed chirping and catcalling. We reached the end of the shelf of conversation and the canyon of sleep dropped off before us. Just before we fell over, my brother spoke up.

"Shawn, why didn't you shout?" he said. "When you found the campfire?"

I wanted to pretend to be asleep, but guessed he would detect that lie. "I was out of breath," I said. It rang so false he didn't even bother with a reply.

We found the footprint next morning. It was in a pool of direct sunlight, which we hadn't seen for days. On the ground the corpses of two trees stretched out, surrounded by reddish saplings struggling to seize the sunlight. Kyle high-stepped over the plants and rubbernecked under a trunk. When he yelped, my heart slid hard. Underneath the trunk, sheltered from the rain, he pointed at the imprint of a sneaker. I checked my brother's shoeprint, just to make sure he hadn't planted it, but the patterns differed.

"Good thing I found this one," Kyle said, hurling a hard glance at me.

"Five days in, five days out," I said. "That's the math. And your shoulder is looking nasty. I'm going to have to carry you out."

"We can hightail it back once we find them," my brother said. "We are so close."

"Unless we get lost on the way back. Your compass skills—"

"Have you hid any other clues from me?"

I made a noise of disgust.

He had already moved from the clearing. "Don't sabotage me like you've sabotaged your life."

A pocket of air enlarged in my throat. I wanted to snap the branches of every visible plant. "This from a guy who ruined a whole company?"

"At least I had a company," he said. "What would you ruin? A mixed drink?"

He walked away quickly. If those bites didn't kill that son of a bitch, I might strangle him as he slept.

Hours later, following the best traditions of our family, he pretended nothing had happened and started talking about James and John. He mentioned how funny they would look with enormous beards, and said their love for each other surpassed the love of most marriages. He namedropped Congo and Madagascar as the most recent places they'd visited to evangelize natives. They did so believing that reaching the last people group with the gospel would inaugurate the end times, which would get them whisked up to heaven. My brother didn't even bother to mock this insane idea. No wonder he wasn't ready to give up—he really loved them. It was only a proxy love, love by marriage, but he'd been infected, and I wished I could slip him a drug to help him detach.

As we approached the center of the mountains, the canopy sifted out even more light. The plants pressed in, denser and denser. Everything reeked of fungi, soil, and fur. Some trees oozed a mustard-colored caulking that looked poisonous and moss graffitied tree trunks. Kyle made a small noise. He was grimacing while holding his shoulder. When he saw me looking, he straightened up and relaxed his expression.

"I'm out of food," I lied.

"How can you be out of food?" he asked. He sounded like it hurt to talk.

"I think some animal stole some while we slept. We need to head back, man."

A drop of sweat chased another down his temple. Even though he'd been All-American everything—student, athlete, husband, son—he was reaching his limits now.

"Marie needs her brothers," he said.

Post-lunch, I had no idea how Kyle was choosing our route. The geography didn't offer the obvious markers of streams or hills and he only glanced at the compass sporadically. I considered ditching him. While he slept, I could take the compass and try to backtrack to the helicopter. But I hadn't written down our course, and besides, I didn't have the heart to abandon him. After all, he was family. Once night fell, he used a flashlight to keep hiking, even after a bat dive-bombed him, even after he fell down several times, until I convinced him that we would miss any clues in the darkness.

We ate by the light of the Sterno until the jelly burned down to an unearthly glow. The meatballs in the freeze-dried spaghetti tasted like soggy Styrofoam, but I could have eaten three more packets. I'd probably lost ten pounds already. My brother couldn't finish his food, and that worried me more than his shoulder. After dinner I helped clean the wound and dress it. The twin bites radiated colors into the veins around them, like a child's drawing of a sun. He needed a doctor. He needed poison control or a lancing.

"How much longer are you going to survive with this?"

"This wouldn't have stopped James or John—"

"Your brothers-in-law are crazy," I said. I'd said it before but it needed repeating.

Kyle snapped a piece of bark using only one hand. "I admire their persistence." And he looked reproachfully at me, as if to emphasize the difference between them and me.

I finished bandaging him up. "Persistent, sure. But how did they feel when they figured out there weren't any natives?"

"How can you be sure there aren't natives?"

"C'mon. Five days and we haven't seen a trace."

"I have faith they're here somewhere," he said. That sounded odd coming from him. It sounded like the phrase of a missionary.

A pair of moths orbited the dying light of the Sterno can. "With brothers like that, I'm amazed Marie ended up semi-normal."

"She's come back to her religious roots recently. Because of our struggle."

My tongue felt thick in my mouth. "I didn't know you were having marriage problems."

"Not that kind of struggle," he said. "God, you are so dense. Why do you think we haven't had kids?"

As I realized it, I did feel a little stupid. But I'd spent my sexual life fighting against pregnancy, believing that a single slip of the rubber would pop a belly. I'd seen it in my life, in my friends' lives, the way fertility spread like bamboo, so yes, I struggled to imagine striving for it without getting results.

He shook his head. "Maybe you should go back to school. Finish your BA and start a career. You're going to turn thirty soon. Time to get smart and do something with your life."

"At least I'm happy."

"Of course you're happy," he said. "You lounge through life but things still work out. You're the laziest, luckiest bastard I know. Well, guess what? Not everybody has that kind of luck. Some of us work our asses off trying to build a career and a family and it all breaks up on us, and when it does, we're left staring at people like you, people who live on the welfare of the universe, just coasting along without any sense of drive. Do you even know what it takes to build a business like mine? The hours? The dedication? Do you even know what it costs to build your life into something you're proud of?"

The insects joined his judgment, shrilly condemning me. Only one person within hundreds of kilometers, and he hated me. "With the hours you worked, no wonder you couldn't get pregnant," I said. "Were you even home long enough to fuck her?"

"You goddamn monster. You goddamn—" He kept flexing and tightening his hands.

It was too cruel of a thing to say and I regretted it. Before he decided to get violent, I crawled into the fortress of the tent and zipped it up. When he came inside an hour later, I was still awake. All of his movements sounded abrupt and forceful. That night, as we tried to fall asleep, the sound of our breathing fenced—his with deeper, angry thrusts, mine with shallow, rapid parries. Our tent seemed unusually small.

We woke without speaking and hiked without speaking, going farther in and deeper in. Fog suffocated the trees.

Birds, ferns, and vines ghosted into view and out again. The ground became a weave of gnarled roots, choking out the soil and snaking along the surface like sea monsters painted on old globes. Every step sabotaged our chances to make it back to the bog for the rendezvous, condemning us to the same fate as the missionaries. We were six days in, with only four days to get out, and that math tormented me. I calculated how fast I could move carrying my brother, and wondered whether I could even save myself.

"We need to turn back," I said.

A chain of butterflies fluttered past.

"The helicopter will leave without us," I said.

Monkeys chattered up in the canopy, concealed by the fog.

"We won't help anyone by dying out here," I said.

We hurdled a series of decomposing logs.

"Marie will forgive you," I said.

"No, she won't," he said. "They're like children to her." He tripped over a log and didn't get up. I rolled him over and dug mud from his mouth, and he began coughing like he'd been brought back to life.

"Give up," I said. "Just give up. We've done our best."

He propped himself up on his good arm. His face contorted into an expression that people usually don't allow themselves, one that transcribes their deepest emotions onto their face: "I don't know how I'm related to you."

He meant it as a knockout blow. All the bitterness he'd held against me was bundled up with those words. And he was right—I didn't belong in our family. I didn't match. I was the one who couldn't accomplish anything, who had failed to even attempt anything. But strangely, his words didn't hurt me. He was half-dead in my arms, and for once I was the brother on top. Now, maybe for the first time, he needed me. "This is how we're related," I said. "I'm the family member that's going to save your life. Not your wife, not our parents, not James or John. Just me. I'm going to throw you over my shoulder and get you home alive."

As I spoke his eyes flickered with what I had always craved: some respect. I had looked everywhere for that, in the company of potheads and the compliments of strangers, even though I thought it could only come from family. And then it was gone. He stared perpendicular to me, his expression showing the journey of processing my words, until his concentration shifted and a look of bewilderment conquered his face. I looked where he was looking, and saw, through a cleft in the trees, a patch of red.

We found their tent in the clearing. Next to the tent sat two sleeping bags and two backpacks. One side of the tent bowed gently as air shifted against it, then relaxed to its former shape, like an organ inflating and contracting. Although the entryway was zipped from top to bottom, the lips of the zipper had separated for a space in the middle, leaving a small slit. Dewdrops from the early morning fog moistened the front.

My brother had one foot in front as though willing himself forward, but his upper body leaned back. He indicated with a finger that I should open the tent. I declined. He needed to witness this truth for himself. He moved forward as if being propelled. Instead of unzipping it from the bottom, he grabbed both sides of the slit and pulled. The flaps parted and Kyle stepped back.

"How can it be empty?" he said. "It can't be empty."

I was a little relieved. As much as I wanted closure, I didn't want to confront corpses.

"We have to keep trying," he said, slumping to the ground. "They might be out here somewhere." His eyes looked feral.

I volunteered to search the area. I flailed through the surrounding flora, flushing out squadrons of birds that squawked their disapproval. As I got farther away, I heard him shouting from the camp, but only the outline of the words and not their sense. When I swung in closer, I realized he was shouting their names, asking them to think of their sister, to consider what their disappearance had meant to their parents. Asking them what was so important out here that they would sacrifice their lives. He began cursing them with every profanity he could dredge up. "I need you," he kept yelling into the unforgiving leaves. I searched the surrounding area for an hour, and came back to find him halfway inside the tent, the debris of their backpacks surrounding him.

He read my report in my eyes. "If they're dead, where are their bodies?" he said. "Where are they? They couldn't just vanish."

"Kyle. Kyle. You've got to let them go." I said it as kindly as I could, but the words still fell hard. He ignored me. We sat until I decided it was time for a fire. I felled a tree with the travel hatchet and lit the wood. Black smoke spiraled upwards, sap popped, and froth bubbled from the ends of branches.

When my brother staggered up and grabbed the hatchet, I was surprised he still had the energy. He attacked a tree, each chop exhausting him, until he'd cut off a single branch. By now the fire had grown to a bonfire, with the uppermost flames reaching the height of a man. Cradling the branch with his good arm, he twisted his torso like a shot-putter to hurl it into the flames, and it tumbled from the apex to the embers, where it lit and burned. Perhaps it was the way it landed, for in the shroud of flames the wood created the form of a tiny, budding body. I could make out a head, chest, arms. The figure looked fragile and translucent in the flickering light. When a wet branch popped, launching fireworks of sparks, the edges of the fire blurred into the vegetation as my brother darkened into silhouette, and when I refocused, the wood was only wood and my brother small before it.

He sat beside me, sweating profusely, and we watched the fire burn. He looked like a man who didn't cry but had reached the point where crying was required of him. He was much smaller than I'd ever seen him, and I felt our roles reverse, as though I was the older brother, the one meant to lead the way and coach him through the miseries of life. We weren't a hugging family but I put an arm around him. He remained stiff before finally relaxing into my embrace.

With my nose close to his shoulder, I could smell his sour and rotten stench. After I helped remove his shirt, the light of the fire revealed the full infection. So I did what I should have done days ago: I took out the knife. It had a five-inch blade that snapped upright with an ominous click. Then I arranged the supplies on my backpack: gauze to stop the bleeding, a bottle of disinfectant, two large bandages.

He watched the proceedings with frightened eyes. "I'm going to save you," I said.

"Let's wait a little," he whispered.

We waited, watching the smoke curl from the flames. Coals pulsed from rose to ruby to nova, like hearts pumping energy to the limits of the fire. I kept the knife in my hand, propping it on my knee. My brother looked at the canopy as if searching for a miraculous salvation, but he should have been looking next to him.

"Remember how we always teamed up for flashlight fights?" he said. "How we had all those hand signals? We'd always attack the enemy base together, one of us crawling through the juniper bushes, the other creeping behind the hedge. What were we? Ten and twelve? Those were good times. God, we really liked each other back then."

I smiled, but not because it was true. I didn't remember a single game we'd played on the same team—we were always enemies, with me playing defense, and whenever he tried to capture our base I'd nail him with my light. He was always frustrated with how I'd sit back in a secret spot and wait to knock off anyone who came, while he worked so hard to infiltrate and kept failing. But I wanted him to remember it his way. I wanted him to rewrite his memories until all the dark history of our relationship had been whitewashed. "Those sure were great times," I said. "Now lay down."

He lay down in front of the fire, and I knelt beside him. I'd never cut anyone and worried the blood would make me woozy. Should I approach it gingerly or go quick? I gave him a piece of bark to bite. When I slapped the blade against my palm three times, he nodded at me, but before I could cut he spat out the bark and said, "Wait." He pressed his fingers into his temples, wearing an expression like a revelation, as though someone had whispered the password to the universe.

"James and John didn't die," he said in a voice fringed with awe. "They were caught up. Just like they hoped they would be."

It was a crazy thing to say, and I knew he couldn't have meant it. The pain must have made him delirious. But he still had that radiant look, and he was looking at a place far beyond the canopy.

He grabbed my calf and squeezed tight. "Believe me," he said. "Believe it."

I smiled falsely at him, the way I'd smile at a stranger's crying baby. Then I cut deeply into his wound.

This was the plan: he wouldn't lose too much blood and the infection wouldn't spread. The compass would work and I would carry him when he got weak and we would reach the bog in time. The helicopter would retrace our flight over the shag-carpet mountains, returning to the village with the dirt strip where the four-seat Cessna would buzz us back to Jayapura. Local doctors would save him. Our jet would layover in Hawaii before returning us home. His wife would make peace with the loss of her brothers, and he would stop accepting crazy beliefs and release the pressure he kept on himself to shape the perfect family and perfect career, and maybe I would even get a brother back, a brother who wouldn't always hold me up to the standard of what I had done and not done. I could see it all unspool before me, the perfect plan for the future, but deep in my gut I knew it wouldn't happen that way.

Tentmaking in Tehran

I met the man who called himself Mr. Hamidi in a teahouse in southern Tehran. At the teahouse, I lay on the couch under a watercolor painting of Ferdowsi square and drank tea through a sugar chunk. Ceiling fans chopped at the heat and a stereo coughed out Gypsy Kings. This was my favorite teahouse because of the easy route of escape—the kitchen exit led to busy streets.

When Mr. Hamidi arrived, I identified him by the blue shirt. I told people what to wear but never what I would wear. He was young and Islamic stubble shaded his cheeks. He paused inside the entrance, so the sun clung to the back of his jeans while his head broke into the dark room. I watched his eyes. They looked only at the booths. Once, I met with someone who looked at the exits before the tables, and I had left without meeting him.

I stood and approached him.

"Mr. Raad?" he asked, which was the name I used in this country. "*Salaam.*"

Mr. Hamidi wore a smile so clean I suspected it. He was unmarried and claimed he worked as a cook in an Italian restaurant. In Dubai, where he stayed for one year, he learned how to cook Italian food. He listed many pastas: tortetelli, farfalle, rotelle, rigatoni. He wanted to create a new pasta, an Iranian pasta, for the glory of Persia. If he wanted to increase the glory of Persia he should make one in the shape of the bomb, I thought. While we talked, we ate dizi. My bowl needed more spice. My smart, kind, beautiful friend Yu, who was an excellent cook, made me spicier food. Mr. Hamidi praised my Farsi, and I taught him the Thai word for tea. We lowered our voices and discussed what he knew of Christianity. He knew little but was excited. He confessed he was not a good Muslim. Twice he cracked his knuckles all at once by squeezing one fist with the other hand, and the cracks were frightening.

"Jesus is Great," he kept saying, as if this was a crazy idea. Perhaps he was not seeking to betray me. I told him how the Qur'an did not give grace to evildoers, but how it pointed to the grace of Christ. The music and other people made eavesdropping difficult, but Mr. Hamidi still glanced around nervously. Even though I was cautious about new members like Mr. Hamidi, his interest excited me. I had not scored a convert since my arrival seven months ago, and Mr. Hamidi was on the edge. I imagined guiding him to the crowds on the clouds.

I lit a Homa cigarette and he did the same. I hated smoking but it helped calm my Iranian friends. If this teahouse were safe, I would want Yu here with me. Mr. Hamidi started talking about the West, which he did not like because America bullied his country. "They are like nervous children pretending to be parents," he said. He kept railing against America the hypocrite, only making an exception for some of their music and movies, and I kept my face sympathetic in order to avoid betraying myself. I had worked hard to erase my four years of America from my speech and to only mention Thailand. When he finished, I sympathized by saying that in Thailand, the farangs— especially Americans—danced over our beaches wearing skimpy swimsuits, and older Thais complained. We agreed: Americans pushed themselves into every country.

Mr. Hamidi insisted on paying for the meal three times. I refused three times. When he insisted a fourth time I knew he meant it, so I let him pay. He took out many coins—it seemed like thirty or more—to make the bill.

We stepped into the aggressive daylight. "I want to join a group," he said.

In each group, we studied the Word and hummed worship songs low enough that curious neighbors could not hear. My goal was to grow the group but every new member might be a spy. "It is best if you and I talk again," I said.

When we left, we walked opposite ways. But after a few steps, I stopped. I had a suspicion. A suspicion of nothing. Still, I stood before a man selling hot beets and watched Mr. Hamidi. He walked head down, blinded by concentration, past the girls in pink chador and the flowering Cypress trees. I watched until he was nearly gone and thought I had watched for no reason. But before I turned away, he stopped in front of a charity box for Islamic offerings. They were blue, framed by yellow hands, and decorated many street corners. Mr. Hamidi dug into his pocket, searching for a coin. Finally, he found one, slipped it into the box, and continued. A shiver seized my legs. I thought that the teahouse man and the man giving money were not the same man.

In the afternoon, the wind slid off the Alborz mountains and delivered the smell of laundry from the textile factory next door. Forklifts grunted, lifting pallets of halal dolls, and workmen shouted insults as complex as poems. Inside the office, Ji worked. He was a tentmaker like me, a man working to support his ministry. While other missionaries lived on funding, their salaries determined by the price of a McDonald's hamburger in their host country, we had to find jobs. Ji started this company as a front but soon made it real. He had always planned to minister in Iran, while I had fallen into this country by accident, because the missionary institute in India needed one spot filled in the Farsi class. Ji was having a coughing fit, which had gotten more frequent after three years in Tehran's exhausting air. Despite the coughing, his eyes never left the computer screen. Many days he worked without breaks for twelve hours.

"I worry about this one," I said in Farsi. "He acted like he was acting."

"You know why I am not in Evin prison?" Ji said, leaning toward the computer screen. "Because I am anxious for nothing. I act as though I am not doing anything illegal."

"I get tired from acting," I said.

Ji pinched his chin, which he did when worried. "Why do you think he is a spy?"

I told him about the charity box.

"If he is a good Muslim, he will be a good Christian."

"If he is too good a Muslim, he will betray Christians."

Ji turned from the computer. "You worried too much about the last man and he never joined."

"So I shouldn't be careful?"

"No, be careful. Be very careful. Remember Nadarkhani." This man of faith was arrested and threatened with execution. And six months ago in Qom the government arrested a homosexual, a Christian, and a man on the wrong side of politics. If foreigners like ourselves were caught, we would be charged with blasphemy or spying.

Ji worked for a few more hours until he had another coughing fit and went home to his wife Yu. Twice a week I went home with him, and he and Yu sat close and laughed in unison so when I joined their laughter it sounded like an echo. It made me sad that Ji was so in love with Yu, because I wouldn't want to hurt him. That night I left the warehouse late, when the subway was empty except for laughing girls with bright headscarves.

In my apartment building the stairwell smelled like *esphand*, the seeds burned to ward off evil spirits. My door only had two locks, which did not seem enough. Once in the apartment, I kept the lights off until I had checked the alley from the back window. My refrigerator had little food so I ate only rice and fruit. I set an empty plate across from me. At the language institute in India where they trained me, if an extra chair was available in a meeting, they would joke it was for the prophet Elijah. So this was Elijah's plate. As I ate I talked to him: "Elijah, this city smells like a bus fart." I wanted to talk to people back home in Thailand, but worried that the government would listen to my calls and arrest me. I knew the internet was monitored so I did not send emails.

I was not always a nervous man. At the language institute in India, I was known as Mr. Funny. I plucked many jokes from the Word. "What person in the Word did not have a father or mother? Joshua, son of Nun." That always made people laugh. At parties, I was the one who sang too loudly and made funny gestures. But in Iran, keeping so many secrets made me tight. Ji said, "You are too anxious, Raad." Then he quoted from the Word about not being anxious for tomorrow. But I could not help being anxious, and convinced myself it was holy because otherwise I could not stay out of prison.

The smell of *esphand* had leaked from the hallway. I turned off the lights and checked the alleyway. The muezzin down the street wailed Islamic prayers, which reminded me to pray Christian prayers. When I crawled into bed, I prayed that I would not dream of Mr. Hamidi or Evin prison, but of the taste of the sea and colors of my childhood.

My Tuesday meeting, near the park in Naziabad, was in an Eastern-bloc apartment next to a white building with Greek

columns. I had been leading the group for several months
and most of them were strong believers. Still, I had not told
any of them about my time cleaning offices in New York. I
talked only of the rambutans and water lizards of Thailand.
Once I talked so much about currents and tides and brine,
recalling my childhood on my father's fishing boat in Ko
Chang, that the men checked my neck for gills.

Usually I approached this meeting by the blue subway
line. But since I had given the Word to a man on the West
side of the city, I took the red line and walked through the
park. On the park rim, I bought a cup of rose ice cream
from a man selling them off the back of his motorbike.

At first I did not pay much attention to the beggar, who
sat on the ground opposite the apartment with a small box
for change and whose legs ended at the knees. The war
with Iraq had required the sacrifice of many legs, just like
the war in Cambodia. The beggar held a string of green
beads. Twice every minute, after finishing his prayer, he
shifted a bead from one side to the other. At first I thought
his eyes were closed, but when he turned his head to look at
someone I realized he was only pretending.

It seemed strange he would sit so close to our meeting
place. Why not the grass? And honest people do not pretend
to close their eyes. As one of the men of the meeting entered
the apartment, the beggar thumbed a green bead. He did
not slide another until a second man entered. Despite the
rose ice cream, I began to sweat. He was perfect because no
one would suspect a beggar. And what would happen when
all the men arrived and the beads were pushed to one side?
I imagined a van pulling up and men jumping out and
shoving us into the van and no one hearing from us again.

I called the Iranian leader I had been training.

"Mr. Raad, when are you arriving?" he asked. I realized
that if I told him about the green bead man, the group

would spill out and walk quickly and stare at the beggar, and their fear would stink in the streets. So I said, "I am sick." I told him to cancel the meeting.

"We will stay and have tea," he said.

"No, send everyone home," I said. Then I saw Mr. Hamidi. He walked on the rim of the park. Even though the air had begun to thicken into night, I could see he had the same blue jeans, gray shirt and firm legs. His presence was very suspicious. Perhaps he was helping the beggar. Though the two did not exchange glances, this only confirmed their talents for secrecy.

Mr. Hamidi stepped off the sidewalk and cars swerved before him and motorcycles after. Of course I followed. What else was I to do? I needed to protect myself and the meetings. My throat grew small and my breath quick.

He went into an alley and I followed, even though it made me nervous. Alleys were for drug pushers, not tentmakers. Even though the alley curved, blocking my view of him, I could hear his sandals slap the ground. Someone whistled—a warning whistle? We exited onto a main street. I looked both ways and could not find him. Wait—in the distance, his back. I walked past an old door with a men's knocker on one side and a women's knocker on the other, and Mr. Hamidi turned on the street next to the Dark Owl teahouse. I hurried after him, doubting myself. What would I do if I caught him? No, I did not want to catch him. I just wanted proof. Proof that he was not who he said he was. Proof that I was not being anxious and suspicious.

The street poured through a brick arch into a broad square. A fountain sprayed in the middle. A couple touched briefly, then thought better of it. On the far end, topped by a dome, double doors led into a mosque where men bowed and rose, bowed and rose. I could not see Mr. Hamidi. The square was wide and he could not have crossed it. Unless he had run, there was nowhere he could have gone. It was as if he had disappeared into the air. I had lost him. No, he had lost me. I was turning in a large square, looking for a man I had met once and only followed because he might be tricking me, and I was now lost.

While Yu cooked with Chinese spices and hot oil, Ji and I played Go, placing our white and black stones on the grid. Ji kept surrounding and trapping my stones, and I could not escape. He played the game not with love but with longing for the place it reminded him of.

One month after I arrived in Tehran, Ji returned to China and came back with a wife. Yu was four or seven years younger. Either I had misheard or they had told me different numbers. She often massaged the top of Ji's neck as though she loved that part of his body more than any other. And when they sat, he rubbed small circles on her knee as if polishing a valuable vase. Yu's sneezes sounded petite. They were identical to the sneezes of my former girlfriend in New York. I loved this girl, but she did not want to return to Thailand or be a tentmaker, and so we parted on bad terms.

"Food," Yu announced in Farsi, bringing three dishes to the table in quick order, and Ji nodded to confirm her pronunciation. Ji praised his wife often, and at the warehouse he never complained about her. In his view she was a holy object without flaw. I found her very beautiful because of how she treated Ji. To respect Ji, I had tried to reduce the frequency of my thoughts of her, but this effort failed.

After Ji's blessing, we ate. Even though my tongue longed for Thai flavors, Yu made tasty food. Breaded chicken and vegetable dumplings and bok choy with ginger and garlic. She looked at the food with shy pride.

"Sleeping? Eating?" Yu asked me in Farsi. When she did not know the words, she spoke in Chinese and Ji translated it into Farsi. And when I did not know the word in Farsi, I repeated the word in Thai to loosen my memory. With all these languages colliding, we laughed often.

"I sleep okay," I said. I mimed the phrase by tilting my hand back and forth. "There are many things to be nervous about."

Yu looked at her husband with worry. She knew any danger would spill onto him.

Ji swallowed a bite of bok choy. "You are still nervous about the new man," he said.

"He followed me to the Tuesday meeting."

Ji and Yu stiffened. "You are sure it was him?" Ji asked. "You are sure?"

"Perhaps it was not him. It was dark and he disappeared. But he wore the same jeans and his body looked the same."

"The same jeans?"

"Blue. Loose on his body."

Ji settled back in his chair and looked at the ceiling. "Let me tell you a story," he said. "A farmer lived in the hills."

"In China?" I asked.

"One day there was a revolution," he continued. "A man in uniform came to town and told the villagers that the four olds were now forbidden—old customs, old cultures, old habits, old ideas. Forbidden! Killing these old ideas meant that the villagers could no longer keep their lineage books. But the farmer did not want to burn his lineage book. He respected his family too much. However, soldiers went to every house, and if they found any example of the four olds, they burned the house and beat the owner.

"So the farmer bought wood and built a secret space beneath his house. Also, he stopped bragging about his family history and spent time in the square, where he could see the soldiers coming. When others spoke about the four olds, he spoke harshly so no one suspected him, even though before he never supported the revolution.

"Then the official and soldiers came to the house. The official said everyone knew the farmer had bought wood and changed his talk, which meant he was hiding. So the soldiers found the secret space, burned the lineage book, and sent the man to a camp."

Ji looked sad. I suspected the story was not untrue. "See? It was not the search that caused worry, but worry that caused the search." He eyed me across the table. "Look at your shoulders," he said, and I dropped them. When he rubbed a finger over my eyebrow, folds fell from my face. "Are you sure you are called?"

This scared me. No one had ever questioned my calling. "Yes, yes, of course," I said. But maybe he was right. My numbers were so low it made me doubt. Ji had converted households and ran five meetings. I had converted no one and ran only one meeting. Which made me feel like Mr. Hamidi was important. I wanted him to be safe so he could be converted. He seemed on the rim.

"Meet him one more time," Ji said. "Then, if you still worry…" He fluttered his hand into the air like a spooked bird.

After dinner, Ji tried to clean the dishes but Yu, showing her usual eagerness to serve, pushed him from the kitchen. Ji and I retreated to the general room.

"Did you hear the news today?" Ji asked. He pretended to hold an object, clicking his tongue as he stuck it to a surface, and flung his hand out while making the noise of violence.

We had talked about this warfare. Men on a motorbike stuck a bomb to the door of a scientist's vehicle, one of the scientists working on the bomb. Some months ago, in the center of the city, I found plastic bits at my feet. I knelt and wiped some of the thick dust. It smelled like fireworks. At the nearby water pipe café, an old man with nostril hair like broom bristles announced the events of yesterday. Speaking through exhaled smoke, he said it was higher in pitch than a car crash. From the charred car four men had carried a wounded man. Three of the men had a limb to carry, but the fourth man, the one near where the left leg had been, had nothing to lift.

"It is sad," Ji said. "But the more the Iranians worry about motorcycles with bombs, the less they will worry about men with Bibles."

"Small bombs can't fight big bombs forever," I said. "And the Qur'an cannot keep the Bible out forever."

"The Iranians worry about the wrong thing," Ji said. "The most dangerous weapon is not bombs or tentmakers but culture. Young people here have sold their hearts to Hollywood and rock music and Coke. It changes them. Now, even some Basij sell alcohol rather than pouring it out."

"But we also change culture."

"We are not changing culture. We are changing hearts," Ji said. "The human heart is the biggest bomb. You light the fuse and a whole country changes."

Ji began coughing, and when he couldn't stop he took a cylinder from his pocket and squeezed a blast into his mouth. He began breathing easier. "Good air," he said, showing it to me.

When Yu handed me a dish with leftovers, our fingers touched. She sat next to her husband, eager to hear our conversation. She rubbed the hair on the back of Ji's head and Ji made circles on Yu's knee. They were a monument to happiness. In a gap in our conversation, Yu turned toward her husband with reverence in her eyes, and he smiled as though newly aware of himself as an object of love. I did not know whether I would ever reach that happiness, but closed my eyes and hoped some would drift to me.

Before siesta on Monday, I walked to my market, the one next to the mural praising the man with a bomb on his chest.

I had seen this mural many times but not stopped to examine it. In the mural, the serious man walked with purpose toward a Star of David. Above him was a series of Arabic words, topped by promising clouds. I imagined that same man with the big bomb strapped to his back and thought it was not crazy to worry about such a man. Any sane country should worry about such a man. Such men wanted nothing but the destruction of the Zionists and the great Satan who supported the Zionists. But I wondered if a mural was made about me, whether Iranians would also worry. I imagined a painting of myself walking toward the Azadi Tower with a Bible strapped on my chest, and behind me, connected by ropes, I pulled a Statue of Liberty with the face of a skeleton and American movies with loose women. Some Iranians would fear that and I could understand why.

Inside the market several women wore their headscarves back, teasing men with a strip of hair. I was certain their shampoo would not smell as good as Yu's. Unfortunately, the market did not carry Thai curry paste, so I bought Indian paste, the one closest in taste.

"Mr. Raad!"

I jumped, startled. It was Mr. Hamidi. He had Persian pudding and Coca-Cola in his basket.

"You live close?" I said.

"No, but I was nearby." He asked about my work.

I mentioned meetings but did not say locations. Then I thought of a clever test. "What did you do two nights ago?"

"Two nights ago?" He frowned and stalled, as if to make up an excuse. "I cooked for the restaurant. And my sauce that night was wonderful. I used a technique I learned in Beirut."

"I thought you learned to cook in Dubai."

He looked confused. "Dubai? Oh, yes. Dubai for a year, Lebanon for a year."

"And where is your restaurant?"

He said a place that was not near the park or the square. Perhaps it had not been him.

"We should meet again?" he said.

I was wary but could not refuse. I suggested the same teahouse, but he disagreed. "No, the Namazi garden. It is beautiful now, with the flowers."

"I will come," I said. At the time it might have been a lie.

"And I have two friends you should meet. They want to hear your beliefs."

I should have been excited by this news, since it was hard to reach people, but I nodded without enthusiasm. Then he said, "May God protect you," and this time I did not watch as he walked away.

On the walk home, the bulky bags straining my arms, I wondered if Mr. Hamidi had staged that meeting. Since I went to the store every Monday, it would not be hard to arrange. As the pink and yellow buses passed, blowing exhaust in my face, I felt like smoking a Homa cigarette.

The next morning I took the subway to Ji's apartment, timing it so Ji would have left for the warehouse. When I knocked, sounds came from the apartment but the door did not open. When it did, Yu opened it only a slit. She was wearing a long dress with modest sleeves, and the fabric had not yet adjusted to her body. I gave her my excuse for coming: the dish that had contained leftovers. She took it and I waited until she invited me for tea.

"Give Ji?" she asked, holding up the dish and looking confused.

"I decided to give it to you. Ji breaks too many things."

I was joking but the language missed her. So I pretended it was not funny.

She moved around the kitchen with the authority of someone who had fully accepted her new role. Ji had told me their families knew each other, back in China, and Yu had always been a hard worker and never complained. Ji said this as though it was the highest compliment.

Yu held up a jar of sugar and I declined. She held up milk and I declined again. "Work today?" she asked.

I used simple words to talk about the new shipment of toys. After I finished speaking, we let the silence and smiles do our heavy lifting. She made small gestures and I sent them back. We drank our tea often to give our mouths some activity. Even though I had little experience with women, I had always dreamed of being alone with Yu. In my dreams we sat so close our knees bumped and her eyes never left my face and we talked for many hours.

"Ji safe. Yes?" Yu said.

Her worry made her beautiful. A single breath could have toppled her. Every man wanted a woman to worry for him so he could be brave in the face of her worry, and hers was the holiest worry because it was born of love. "We are very careful," I said.

"And you?" she said.

She must have known. How Ji knew the lay of this city, where to find support and where to sidestep, yet I stumbled and groped. "If I disappear, you and Ji should leave," I said. "Don't stay, even if Ji wants to."

She nodded.

"Do you really understand? If they take me, you will leave?"

She said she understood.

"Swear to me."

She said the words for yes and no, surrounded by Chinese words, and I realized she was quoting the Word about not swearing. She paused, put a hand on her stomach, and said, "Yes." This promise satisfied me. But her hand was surprising. It seemed a promise on the soul of her future child. But given the careful way that she moved, perhaps she was already with child. Ji was so talented at producing new men.

We drank the rest of our tea using only child-like phrases that split in the wrong directions. Before we opened the door, I hugged her goodbye. I didn't only want her body close to me but also wanted the feeling of being close. Close enough to someone they would worry for me. My girlfriend in New York had never worried for me, and that was a sign. Yu let go of me before I let go of her, and she offered a smile that started as a secret but grew into a public message.

As I left, she offered a shy wave and I replied with a broad hand, saying goodbye twice. Every step on the stairs sounded hollow, as though it would be the one that broke and let me fall.

At the warehouse Ji worked harder than a deckhand, trying to finish all his accounting before his meetings at night. He had recently started two new groups on the outskirts of the city, both requiring a subway ride long enough to lull him to sleep. Every night he got home late and every morning he left early. I do not know whether Yu ever told him about my visit. He never spoke of it. When I told him of my plan to meet with Mr. Hamidi, he nodded his approval but told me to be careful.

On the day and time, I went to the Namazi garden. Even though my stomach swerved like a frightened fish, I would give Mr. Hamidi one more chance. Under a fig tree, I smoked a Homa cigarette. I needed one to calm my nerves. This was not our meeting place but an area where I could watch for Mr. Hamidi's approach. On the grass where families picnicked, babies walked from mother to father with the uncertainty of wind-up toys.

When Mr. Hamidi appeared, he walked among the Holland roses, sticking his nose in their petals. During a stretch of yellow flowers, he held his hand level and brushed against the tops. They all bounced back except one, whose stem broke. He tore it from the stalk and stuck it into the soil. Never once did he relax his false smile.

Two of his friends joined him. At first I thought they were his friends who wanted to convert, but they wore black and had muscles like Muy Thai heavyweights. Behind them lurked a black car. It reminded me of funeral cars. A lump of pain grew in my chest. When Mr. Hamidi embraced them, his arms were jaws of a trap, cocked and ready to spring. When he released them, he cracked many knuckles at once. Those cracks! They were as loud as slammed doors.

Slumped against a cement wall, I prayed. I was called. This was my mission. I could not let these fears defeat me. I knew what Ji would say. He would say I was being too cautious and my groups would never grow if I did not find members. He would say that my imagination built towers of tragedies that fell and fell. So I tried to scoop up all the scared parts of me and pound them into a hard ball of courage. I tried and tried. But my legs were as useless as the prayer-bead beggar's. I crawled to a bench and smoked another cigarette for so long I worried they would explore the park and find me. So I left. On the subway ride back home, I had low thoughts of myself. Even though I was not the type of person who quit anything, perhaps tentmaking was not for me.

When I reached my apartment, my cell phone rang with double its normal volume. The noise terrified me. It was Yu. She was crying and talking about four cars.

"Four cars what?" I said.

"Morning," she said. "This morning."

She shot out sentences in Chinese and I asked her to speak in Farsi.

"At warehouse," she said. "They take Ji."

She fumbled through her explanation, and I stitched together stray words to make a story. One of the warehouse workers had called her. The government men in black cars, wearing everyday clothes bulging with guns, had pulled up quickly. Without harassing anyone in the warehouse, they put Ji in the fourth car and drove away. Ji had not called her since.

The phone left my ear. Yu kept talking but her voice was small. The nearby minaret blasted its call for prayer, deafening me. Light broke in the windows and sprayed the carpet with glare. Only the bottom lock of my door was fastened. My neighbors were too quiet. Someone yelled in the back alleyway.

I put the phone back to my head and spoke quickly. I told Yu that she should leave the country with me. We could cross the border to Iraq or catch a boat on the Caspian. If she stayed she would not be able to rescue her husband from Evin prison, and they would take her as well. I could not bear the thought of her in prison, I told her. Yu, Yu, I said. I kept saying her name, almost crying it, even though I knew every mention of her name betrayed my affection for her. I hung all my feelings on those two lovely letters, and there was no way she did not understand what I felt for her. I said her name until I could admit to myself what had long been true: I loved her.

The phone remained silent. I said her name once more as a question before I realized the line was dead, and that she had hung up when the phone was away from my ear. An emptiness spread across my chest. My phone dropped to my hip. Those words could never come out of me again, not with the same feeling. But even if she had heard me, I knew my pleas were useless. I knew in my stomach that she would not go. If I were married to my love, I would not leave either.

In my bedroom, I counted my belongings. A mattress beaten down into the shape of a long ashtray. Next to the mattress, two weary books. Near the window, a hump of dirty clothing. There was not much but it seemed like even less now. On the wall I had pinned up the only picture in the house, a picture, not of my parents or of my former girlfriend in New York, but a magazine page of a beach that looked like a Thai beach. The sand was white and held the husks of coconuts. The water rippled with lazy waves. I had often stared at that beach to lift my spirits before falling asleep, but now it seemed like the saddest picture in the world.

As I threw clothes into my suitcase, I felt jealous of Ji. Strange, to be jealous of an imprisoned man, a tortured man. A man torn from his wife, a man cut down in the height of his work. But at least he had risked everything because he was destined for this task. I had risked my life because I was living out someone else's plan for my life, the plan assigned to many good believers, a plan I thought was my own. Maybe it had been my plan when I was younger, but it could not be my plan now. It was time for me to quit.

I stepped outside the apartment carrying a suitcase. In the hallway it felt suspicious to carry the suitcase, so I put the suitcase back inside. Nothing of value, anyways. I started to lock the door out of habit, but stopped. Why should I? I left it unlocked. I paused before I left. The hallway still smelled like *esphand*. The alleyway was just as loud. I would hear the call of the minaret echo in my dreams; I would hear it forever. With nothing but my pockets and shoes, I left that country and never returned.

Down on the Pitch

As time drips through the last-second dregs, we're losing by a point. I'm booking it down the touchline, ball tucked away, grass blurring beneath my feet. Coach's yell hangs in the air: "M.T.! Hustle!" Hustle is our only game plan. The gameshirts mass their ranks and prepare to destroy my body. I sidestep one, but he slows me. Just before the next gameshirt slams into my waist, lifting my feet off the ground and jackknifing my body, I see a freeze-frame of his face, full of grit and intensity, and know he's the one I'll seedplant.

My brother Lobo's hurtling my way so I granny the ball in his direction. His face is twisted up into a snarl, ready to destroy a thousand bodies just to score. As I go to ground, the hot breath of my opponent fouling up what I'm trying to suck in, my brother trusses the rugby ball against his stomach and bulldozes to the edge of the try zone before four gameshirts stop him. The whistle blows. The game dies.

I lead the line to shake hands. If a Geiger counter could register disappointment, it'd go wild. First time we'd actually been close in a game. Now we're 0–8. As Captain, I shoulder my teammates' disappointment. Although we didn't come down under to win, it'd be nice. In the locker room, Coach talks. He has a barrel chest from when he used to strength train professionally, before his distracted spotters let five hundred pounds crush him. Coach doesn't lose his temper like thin coaches because he's too big. He just stabs his index finger at you with his palm facing up.

"Missed tackles?" he asks. He means how many. We don't answer because it's rhetorical, but the tone of his concluding prayer implies he's proud of us. Afterwards, we strip and survey the damage. Our bodies are battlegrounds. Without the insulation of football pads we scratch, we bruise, we break. Casualties mount across our skin and under it. My brother does a cursory check, believing himself invulnerable. When I point to a rose of blood welling up on his thigh and ask if he wants salve, he just laughs and jabs it with a fingernail. I offer salve to everyone else, trying to help them patch up.

Before we meet with the other team for seedplanting, we return to the rooms and Coach orders pizza and breadsticks. We shower and eat. I play cards with the team. Poker, for Aussie pennies. We don't bet more because Coach says Jesus never gambled. "Don't you dare frickin' bankrupt me," Squidface says whenever he pushes all in. I take pity and fold even when I know I'll beat him. Also, when Studbull gets low on chips, I sneak a few into his stacks. Before my father died, he said I practiced a "disabling kindness." At the time I thought the disabling applied to those receiving my kindnesses. Toward the end of the game, Muscles comes and whispers, "M.T., your brother's down."

I know what he means, even though usually I think of the word in terms of sports. I find my brother curled up at the end of the rooms, his back against the stucco. Sunset casts a burnt light on an old, creepy playground.

"I'd be depressed, too, staring at that," I joke, but know it's the wrong move when his face doesn't change. I sit beside him and don't ask what's wrong, because when someone flips as often as he does, and he's been flipping more frequently the last year, it's not circumstances, even though he grabs at reasons.

"I don't know why I came," he says.

I give all the right answers to why he came, like spreading the gospel and serving the needy, even though I know none of them will work. It's getting harder and harder to break him from these states. Sometimes it's hunger, but he just ate. My greatest fear is that he'll wander off in one of these moods and hurt himself, just like our father did. When my brother was in junior high and I was a freshman in high school, our father hurt himself in a permanent way. A week after the funeral, after my brother hadn't eaten for days, my mother and I started seeing bruises peeking out from his clothes. At first we ignored them, but then I opened our bedroom door at the wrong moment and caught him with his hand cocked over his discolored thigh.

"No one's even soul searching," he says.

"But we're planting seeds."

He's wallowing, so far down he can't see the light at the top of the well. I watch the dark thoughts brood in his head, the lips that dam up hateful words. He gets up abruptly and walks away, across the field, toward the dying sun. He doesn't reply when I ask him where he's going, and I imagine him walking away and not coming back, so I run after him and grab him from behind, pinning his arms against his sides. My right hand locks around my left wrist. Less a bear hug, more a wrestler's grip.

"Let me go," he says, squirming.

I twist my face against his spine so he can feel my no.

"I just need to be alone," he says.

But he doesn't need to be alone. Alone is where I'm scared for him to be. And I don't know how it happens, whether he shifts his weight or I throw him down, but we're on the ground. I haven't let go. My left shoulder took the pile-drive of our weights and the brunt force leaves it throbbing. Although my body's still tense, I can feel him start to relax. Anger and sadness ebb from his muscles.

At home, my brother never wanted to get help. Hated doctors, hated pills, even vitamins. But I insisted he visit a specialist before we left. Three meetings for free, a counselor connection through our pews. I was hoping for pills, even though I knew that in our circles they frowned on that. She went over the Word with him, probing his personal life for mistakes. To her, the solution lay in adjusting his actions— pumping up virtue, avoiding wickedness. The counseling didn't help much. After the third meeting, I found him lying on his back on our driveway, arms stretched out, crying. He didn't move, not even when Scruffy licked his tears. For the next week I took him on a pick-me-up tour of theme parks and bowling alleys and miniature golf courses and friend's birthday parties, burning out my wallet, sacrificing all my hard-fought grades. Not that it helped.

On the ground, I move my mouth from his back and ask, "Want some beef jerky?" He loves beef jerky and it always hikes up his spirits, but he doesn't reply. I'm wondering how he's going to survive the rest of this trip. But I'm also thinking about my own limits. There's only so much I can give before I'm empty.

At the pub, a small television perches over the cluster of liquor bottles. The all-male crowd huddles around, and the air smells of cheap beer. The game's between the Sydney rugby team and Brisbane. Everyone cheers for Brisbane, which I mispronounce until corrected: rhymes not with rain but run. Our team gets sodas and sits with the beer-swilling gameshirts. I join my brother and the other team's flanker and captain, the guy who folded me like origami. We talk about sport first, about American football and how it's different from rugby. My brother still seems down but he's recovering, judging by the rate he's mowing through the table peanuts.

This is the part where I get nervous. My throat locks up and my heart gallops. At least it's easier to seedplant when it's a close game, because the opponents still respect you. Finally, I maneuver the conversation toward the pews and ask about their history.

"My parents never touched the stuff," the flanker says. "But my grandmother prayed when someone was about to die."

"My parents neither," the captain says. "My aunt though, once I went to mass with her on Easter. Thought it was bloody ridiculous." The silence hangs. We turn to the tele as a stopgap. It'd be easier to talk about drinking yourself into a quadriplegic state or fiddling a girlfriend, because those things bind men together.

Just as I hope my brother's recovered enough to step in and save me, he does. "When we were little, we sometimes thought it ridiculous, but when our father passed, we went double-time." My brother tells the rest of the story, how we dug into a Baptist church and never pulled a Lot's wife. As he speaks, I wonder what he would have done if I'd let him wander off today. And what business he has telling others about eternal life when he has a hard time hanging onto the life he's got.

When my brother finishes, we search for the right move. Play it too heavy and you lose them. Play it too light and you kick yourself for cowardice. My brother and I take roles: he acts more religious, I lighten things up. We talk about these things until it grows too awkward and then invite them to come to the local pews next Sunday. They both decline but we don't blame them. Maybe next time, with someone else, they'll say yes. Two hours later, once we've sandwiched the religious talk between sport talk, our team leaves. Their team stays: another game on the tele.

On the walk home he's fully recovered, and we sling arms around each other's shoulders. In exaggerated accents, we sing a German bar song that the Aussies from the last team taught us. A bystander would have thought us drunk, and we are drunk. Drunk on the sugar and caffeine, drunk in the lateness of the cool hour, drunk on the feeling that we've done our duty and planted a seed. Most of my happiness is because I see the electricity in his eyes and am glad he's broken out of the dull-socket depression. Despite all of the bruises blooming over our skin and tenderizing our muscles, despite the recent bout of sorrow that swept over my brother, we are frickin' flying on the thrill of hope.

Coach wakes us at six in the morning. My shoulder, the one crushed by my brother's weight, pulses with pain. "Last one in the van plays missionary," Coach says. He means the drill. We get in the van at six thirty—Muscle's the last one; *missionary*, we rib him, playfully—and Coach starts driving for Toowoomba, a university town six hours away. It took Coach a week, but he's finally adjusted to driving on the left side of the road, although his right turns still cut into the median. The white van, owned by Athlete Ministries, is about fifteen years old and stuffing sprouts from the seats. Some belts we tie around our waists because the buckles fail.

On the road, we flirt with a van of pom-poms. They flash batons and wave slinky limbs. One plants a kiss on the window. Lipstick lingers. Studbull fogs up our window and writes, "You are hot." Instead of writing a message myself, I give the other guys a chance. Aussie chicks aren't prettier than girls in other countries, but their accents are delicious. I love when they say "No"—the way they add extra vowels as if savoring the word.

In Toowoomba, gusts sweep across open spaces. The sky stretches so far that clouds bend over the horizon. There's a game field—what they call, and what Coach insists we call, a pitch—that might pass as mediocre in a third-

world country. We don't talk about it, we joust: "Did they
mean to add speed bumps?" "Grass planter had hiccups."
"More gophers than grass." "What herd grazed this to
death?" But we would play on asphalt if the game was on
and Coach flagged us go.

Coach hasn't forgotten about this morning's promise.
Muscles locks into tripod position mid-pitch and the rest
of us line up in the try zone. Boomer yells that Muscles
should take it easy, we're friendly combatants. We run and
try to avoid Muscles' tackles, but he wraps up two before
we reach the other end.

I pretend to congratulate him: "Thanks for not killing us!"

"Go ahead and try!" Lobo shouts. He's always been
confrontational on the field. His nickname Lobotomizer
came from an early scrimmage when he slammed a guy so
hard the guy's baldcap flew off. Then—and it seemed
impossible, according to physics—before the guy met
ground, he hit him a second time, delivering a hospital-
worthy concussion.

The two tackled guys are converted and join Muscles in
the middle, and they try to tackle more of us as we cross
again. Finally, only three of us—Lobo, Chazzy and myself—
are left as unconverted heathens against the rest of the team.
I run close to my brother, to siphon off his would-be
tacklers. Chazzy and I are forced to ground, though not
without trouble. My brother breaks three tackles and stiff-
arms Muscles. He reaches the other side and beats his chest:
head back, mouth open in a long, triumphant yell.

Coach rounded us up from community college football
teams. None of us were going anywhere scholarship-wise,
just playing for the sweat and glory of the game. None of
us knew the others and none of us had played rugby. We
knew how to hit, but not how to tackle without our helmet

first. We knew how to take a hit, but only under the safety of fifteen pounds of pads. Coach taught us the game and we dished out nicknames. When we sent out support letters to our churches and relatives, the money poured in. We were from a few fundie backgrounds—E.V., Baptist, Non-denom—except for Chazzy, who's a hand-raiser.

We've played eight teams and have nine more to go. Six weeks, all in all. Our tag line is "Play the Americans." For some reason that attracts competition. We'll cover the entire East coast, from Melbourne to Cairns, stopping at every podunk college town on the way.

Post-lunch, pre-game, Muscles gives the Word. We have a Word before every game, and Coach didn't want to talk every time, so he made us take turns. Muscles reads a violent passage from Revelation about the judgment of the wicked, and compares it to how it feels good when you hit someone hard. That's a problem of his—he can be too judgmental. Before games he jokes that he's deciding between merely crippling opponents or outright killing them. My decision's the opposite. I try to balance offering mercy and over-extending myself. I guess that's how they started calling me M.T. At one of the circle-jerk hazings of the younger team members, I was being too nice, so someone called me Mother Teresa and it stuck.

The pitch's soggier today. The weatherman here only gives two forecasts—*wet* or *dry*—but he guessed wrong about last night. About thirty people on the sidelines. The gameshirts wear silver-and-blue uniforms and identical boots, the expensive ones, half-kangaroo and half-synthetic. We huddle up and stick our hands together and do our usual pre-game chant.

Before the drop kick, my brother bares his teeth. Not a smile, a snarl. The gameshirts opposite my brother look less frightened than perplexed. Even Muscles thinks it's a little crazy. I once told my brother that teeth baring might make seedplanting more difficult afterwards, but he argued that breaks and concussions don't, as long as they're clean.

When the game starts, the gameshirts score a quick try. Five points. The kick's good too. Seven. They're fast as dogs and wrap us up neat as gifts and they keep on bum rushing our flanks so we can't granny it off quick enough. The pitch is slick and we're tie-dyed in mud. They try again. Twelve points now. I see steam huffing out my brother's ears, even though it's just sweat evaporating. On the next stage of play, we boot it—the wind blowing it past the touchline—and they throw their player higher than us on the line-out. When their runner attempts to thread the gap in our defense, Lobo and I tell him No with a capitol N, smashing into him from opposite sides, me hitting his legs, my brother hitting his chest. The player pinwheels before smashing into the ground. He doesn't get up. A teammate clears his mouth of mud. While the trainer checks his vitals, I apologize to the gameshirts. My brother just paces, muttering to himself and clenching and unclenching his fists. I don't think they appreciate the lack of concern. Finally, his teammates help carry the downed man off.

The gameshirts smell the crazy in my brother and won't let him ride. They keep parting the defensive seas, to lure him in, then collapsing on his chariot with waves of bodies. They're ahead by a good five tries, so it's not about the competition as much as owning the winning side of manhood. After one scrum, my brother comes away with his middle finger at an odd angle. I tell him to go off to get it bandaged, but he just yanks it straight and rips a piece of tape off his uniform to bind it with his ring finger. "Ready," he growls. Next time he's closing in on the try line, leaping to grind the ball into the grass, a gameshirt streaks across the pitch and breaks his face. My brother scores and starts hopping across the try zone, but blood pours from the upper corner of his eye socket. He wipes at it until I guide him off the pitch. His face is dented like a junkyard truck. The blood and mud form a mask. I can't see his left eye because of all the blood, but his right eye still burns with the fire of the game. Coach dabs at the wound. I give a cocked-head look at Coach, which means Take care of him, and Don't let him back in.

We lose for another twenty minutes. Ten minutes left on the clock, and the score divide would be impossible to overcome. I'm streaked with filth and exhausted because, while football gives you breaks between downs, rugby requires marathon stamina. That's when Muscles gets a cleat to his ankle. Their Winger, sprinting at him from the side, slips on the mud and lands a foot squarely on the ankle bulge. It bends inward and Muscles deflates. Coach walks out, but it's a short visit. We carry Muscles off. His ankle hangs awkwardly from his leg. We don't have any more subs, with Fletcher and Cheeky on the injury bench. Coach talks to my brother and I think no, no, no. Over my brother's eye, the white gauze is flushed with blood. I know what Coach is saying: take it easy, just be a body out there so we don't forfeit.

My brother doesn't listen. He jogs out, both teams dumbfounded that he's still walking, and tears into the game. If anything, he's crazier than ever, as if the injuries lit a fuse. Suicide missions into enemy territory, preferring to take the punishment. Bowling into multiple opponents, head down, shoulders cocked. I try to protect him, try to provide opportunities to granny to me, but he refuses. Seems like he wants to be hit until he's nothing, until he's erased himself. When the ball falls dead, I run up to him and ask him what the frick he's doing.

He flashes a face erased of all love and sprints toward the ball carrier, where he's mashed up again, his head wobbling as he barely keeps to his feet. Coach has his arms crossed, head down, as if he can't bear to watch. I know Coach won't take him out because he refuses to forfeit, but I'd gladly take the loss.

As the last seconds tick off, there's a haymaker by a bulky gameshirt that leaves my brother on his back. He's not moving. I jog to him just as the referee blows the game-ending whistle. When I find out he's unconscious, I panic, waving toward the sidelines. Both teams swarm out and the other team's trainer makes sure he's still breathing. Everything's straight, but his brain's blinked out. "Did he hit his head on the last play?" the trainer keeps asking, and I say that I don't know, I don't know. I worry that he's knocked out permanently, and that it was his plan. I see his body stretched out in a wood-paneled box, eyelids respectfully closed. I should have never let him out of my wrestler's grip. Finally his head wags and he comes to.

"Am I here?" he says loudly, his eyes fluttering back and forth.

"What?" I ask. I'm just glad he's conscious. Squidface and I help him stagger to the sidelines.

While Coach talks to us in the locker room, I bind up my brother. Ice for his finger, swollen to a sausage. His hair's caked with blood, because his right ear's half torn off. When I pull the loose flap, his ear bends perpendicular to his skull.

While the rest of the team does seedplanting, we go to the hospital. Muscles comes along for X-rays. I sit on the chair and my brother smears the white butcher paper with his blood. Out in the hall, Coach talks in short sentences about insurance. I peek and see he's pointing with his index, palm up.

"You were crazy out there," I tell my brother.

He digs at a wound on his forearm until I grab his arm to make him stop. He's sullen, trapped in one of his moods. His lack of energy frightens me. It's one of his deep crashes that comes after a bout of expended energy. Just like when my father swing danced with my mother and cooked an elaborate meal of lobster tacos and jalapeño guacamole and hammered together a backyard fort in the dark, and two days later I entered my parents' bedroom to see a foot. It stuck out from behind the bed, twisted into the carpet. It looked broken even though it was not. It didn't seem to belong to my father.

The doctor injects so much local anesthesia I'm afraid my brother's whole body will go numb. Then she takes X-rays of most of his bones, attaches the ear to his head, sets the eye socket, stitches all the split flesh, splints his finger, and gives him crutches for the swollen, sprained ankle and the tweaked knee. I already know as soon as he leaves the hospital he'll refuse to use the crutches. Sign of weakness. I imagine that if I check where arms and legs meet chest and torso, I'd find thick stitches through blue-black skin, barely holding it all together.

We leave the hospital and return to the rooms, where I situate him on his bed. Water within reach, napkins to staunch bleeding, tons of food to pump him back up, books to waste time. I lie down on the opposite bed and start reading a biography of Pistol Pete. The team pounds on the door before pouring in. Squidface says that his ugly face actually improved. Boomer mentions that once his own ear was torn completely off, so Lobo's wounds are mere flesh wounds. Studbull tells him that the next team will probably put him in bed again. They know how it works: if they offer encouragement, it only communicates the opposite.

I'm glad they showed. This is the only way we know how to support, and it's the only type my brother would accept. It's about loyalty, not intimacy. My brother takes it in without any emotion. I know it must take every blade of his strength just to appear neutral.

Before the guys leave, everyone punches various places on his body, preferably places not bleeding or bruised or broken. Boomer pretends to punch my brother's ankle but pulls it at the last second. My brother winces, then twists his face into endurance itself and stiffens himself as if preparing for the blow. "Do it," he says, his eyes closed, fists clenched. "Do it." Boomer slap boxes him instead.

On the way out, Studbull says, "M.T. You coming to the pool hall?" I tell him no, not indicating my brother because that would embarrass him. Squidface tells me I should come. The rest of the guys chime in, begging.

"If you come," Boomer says, "Studbull and I will stage a fake fight. Super frickin' funny."

Despite the team captain love, I refuse to go until my brother says, "You're not my wet nurse. Go." I step outside and quietly tell the rest of the rest of the team I'm not going with them. They understand. They leave and I stay outside with my ear pressed to the door, listening to the creak of the bed, the sound of him pissing. I want to hear sounds but not any of the wrong sounds. When I cough I step away from the door and muffle it. It'd only annoy him to know how much I try to protect him.

When my brother starts his husky and nasal breathing, I slip back in. I stand over his crumpled mass of limbs and want to crawl into his bed and hug him. It's not my heart that hurts, it's my lungs and stomach and kidneys, burning with pity and love and worry. If he doesn't destroy himself he's going to destroy me. With my hands behind my head, I crunch my skull with my forearms, as if trying to squeeze out useful ideas.

Before we came, a friend told me that we'd see different constellations in this hemisphere. The Southern Cross, for starters. Such a wonderful sign of redemption hanging above your head, he said. The first night I looked but couldn't find it. I thought it'd be obvious but I couldn't draw the right lines. I only saw cobwebs of stars. So I navigated through the weeks without any anchoring points in the sky. I felt I was doing the right thing seedplanting, but I couldn't get any direction from above. Tomorrow, I'll continue to flail. My brother and I will sit in a booth slurping soda and try to tell buzzed gameshirts the answers for the deepest part of their being. I just wish those answers came without struggling against forces so deep inside us that nothing can root them out.

In the morning I coax my brother out of bed. He looks monstrous. Blood has seeped into his cheek, leaving a darkened pool to the right of his nose. His ankle has swollen to a softball. He wants to take the orange splint off his finger but I tell him he shouldn't. I help him redress the gauze on a half-dozen injuries.

"Frickin' go back to bed," he says. "You look terrible."

I spent most of the night awake, pacing when I started to droop, afraid he might get up and act rashly.

"You better win the game today," he says.

"The game doesn't matter," I tell him. "You matter. Seedplanting matters."

Surprise crosses his face, shifting into certainty. "You can't protect me," he says.

He's wrong, wrong as always. He refuses to take his crutches.

At breakfast, where teammates spread tar-like Vegemite across toast—an Aussie delicacy, but I can't stand the sour taste—I say hello to Coach. "All right?" he asks, meaning my brother. I suspect he means more than just the physical. I nod without conviction. My brother eats muffins and cinnamon buns. He prefers steak and eggs—once he ate an all-meat diet, insisting fruits and vegetables make you weak— but the restaurant doesn't serve it. For him, food leads to happiness or unhappiness, and it seems the latter's winning. He's slouched back, like all his energy is draining from his spine, and by the time breakfast finishes he's stopped talking. It's a warning: he's going down again.

We go to the game and Coach gives us the usual game plan. On the pitch, we run half-speed drills. The air has that post-rain briskness, and the gameshirts' uniforms of black and gold stand out sharply against the grass. As we ready ourselves pre-kickoff, I watch my brother hobble along the sidelines, nearly bent in half. The Richter scale of his pain must have spiked. I accompany him to the bench and we sit together in silence, as if no one else is there, watching the pitch. Boomer kisses the toe of his cleat for luck and Muscles dances figure eights around two balls. The gameshirts feint and granny. Every body on that field has a built-up charge, like static electricity, because of the looming violence. I can already sense the games to come, on and off the field, and violence to come, violence we will do to others and violence we will do to ourselves. It scares me enough to drape a protective arm around my brother. It's not like us to hug. Normally he avoids any touches other than forceful ones. And under this one, his shoulders tense.

"You've never helped me," my brother says. "I feel like I'm alone in this."

Liquid burns high in my throat. I think some of my key organs have ruptured. My brother just X-rays the grass. Scratches his Frankenstein ear. Even though it's just his sickness talking, that doesn't cushion the blow. I unhook my arm from around his shoulder and stand up from the bench. I'm about to blow up, to checklist the hundreds of ways I've let him use my body and money and time as a flotation device, and to ask him to name a time in the last year when he's helped me. But to prevent myself from saying anything rash, I escape to the pitch, ripping my cleats into the grass, and join the forming huddle.

Coach speaks in short sentences and points at us with his palm up to show he's serious. Because of my brother's words throbbing in my ears, I hear nothing of what Coach says, except for when he drops our 0–9 record. For motivation. My team wears game faces as they sneak glances at the other team's crisp exercises and gleaming uniforms, and I wonder how many think we'll always be losers. The huddle feels incomplete without Lobo. His energy lit our team's fuse. On the sideline, my brother bumbles about, trying to reach the water jug. When he puts weight on the less injured foot, he winces. Without crutches he's disabled.

Coach finishes his speech and looks to me as team captain. Everyone looks to me. It's my time to stoke up the troops with our pre-game ritual, but I can't do it. At least I can't do it alone. I jog to the sidelines. Before my brother can realize my intention, I scoop him up like a bride. His hairy legs rough up my forearms and the back of his shirt bunches under my other arm.

"What the frick!" he says. "Put me down."

But I don't put him down. I carry him toward the team. The pitch gleams in Technicolor and the sun stabs through the clouds like the second coming. I'm halfway there and already breathing like I need a third lung. My brother looks away from me as if he can't bear the shame, but his arm loops around my neck. Coach and the team stares like we're coming down the aisle. Even the gameshirts stop to watch. My arms burn and my lower back aches but I can handle it. I feel strong, strong enough to carry him across the field and into the airport and back to home and through the rest of his life. I carry him to the center of the circle and the team lifts hands into a teepee above us.

"What are you going to do?" I yell right past my brother's face to the rest of the team.

"Hustle!"

"What are you going to do?"

"Hustle! Hustle! Hustle!"

And with every shout we jump, hands in the air. Shoulders spar with shoulders. Chests jostle backs. Burdened by the weight of my brother, I can only bob up and down. The team shouts faster and jumps faster until the speed whips out of control. "Hustle! Hustle! Hustle!" Behind me someone screams, deafening my right ear. Spit catapults from mouths. Arms crash into arms. We've lost every game and failed so many seedplantings and still we believe. We have faith, faith in our endurance, that our endurance will matter. The word hustle starts to disintegrate. Now it's just a guttural roar. A grunt of determination. The armpits of these fifteen men smell like victory. I feel that in this game, despite all our losses, we will be winners. "Hustle! Hustle! Hustle!" The circle gives me power. My brother is suddenly light in my arms, so I crouch low and blast up. I gain so much air it feels like flight. My head reaches the canopy of hands, a thicket of beige fingers clouding my vision. The upward momentum flings my brother from my arms. He's a finger away but it feels like a canyon. His eyes flare; he must feel like I've thrown him. But he needs to know—he must believe—that when he comes back down I will be there to catch him.

You Will Shout My Name

At the age of twenty-six, while drinking coffee in his Los Angeles studio, Saul Weston experienced his first attack of Tourettes. One moment he was eating oatmeal with allspice and blueberries, and the next moment he heard his voice shouting. He had not meant to shout. He'd startled himself. Even more disturbing was what he had shouted. Given his personal beliefs, it was the most offensive thing he could imagine coming from his mouth. At a tremendous volume he had shouted, "God Will Save You!"

Saul examined his throat in the mirror, but it didn't show anything strange. Was there such a thing as adult-onset Tourettes? He had never heard of it before. He scanned his bookshelf as though the philosophy titles and travel guides to West African countries might provide answers, because he'd always consulted books for the answers in his life, but he sensed this type of problem was beyond the scope of books. He wondered: why *those* words? Why would he say something like *that*? He wasn't religious. He didn't even believe in God.

Gwen would have found it funny. His younger sister, who had died of brain cancer three months ago, had discussions with him in the hospital about the divine and the afterlife. With tubes sticking out from her veins, she would recline the hospital bed and lisp about God. Patiently, because he knew she was dying, he would rebuff her religious ideas, and she would smile and change the subject. Even when they disagreed in their family, they did so politely. But her hackneyed religious ideas disappointed him, and even more disappointing, this did not seem like his sister.

Saul arrived at work worried. Worried because any loud bellow would be heard by the entire company. In his cubicle he studied the feelings in his throat and tongue, wondering if he could devise an early detection device. Perhaps he should choke himself if he felt it coming. Or make himself sneeze. In the morning he worked on a PR campaign to pacify the neighbors near an impending distribution center, even though he didn't believe anything he was writing.

In late afternoon he visited the break room. Two women from human resources, whom he knew only by face, talked in hushed tones while stirring sugar into their tea. As he poured from the coffeepot, the phrase erupted from his throat: "Jesus Died For Your Sins!" He tried to cough at 'sins' but couldn't and so coughed afterwards, jackknifing his body for exaggeration. The women stared at him with surprise and disgust.

"*What* did you say?" the tall one asked.

"What? Nothing. Just coughing."

"I heard you. Clearly."

"Wasn't me. Maybe people passing in the hall."

"Saul," the short one said, surprised. "I never pegged you for a—"

"I'm not," Saul said. "Never. I don't even believe in—"

"We don't need any advice about our families, thank you very little," the tall one said.

"That wasn't me speaking," Saul said. "I didn't even hear what you were talking about."

"And you're too much of a coward to admit it?" the tall one said. "Oh. Oh. That *really* snaps my patience."

"You should be who you are," the short one said. "Even if that is—" And she grimaced.

"Please," Saul said. "Please believe me. Please and I'm sorry."

The short one shook her head as if to settle the pieces of her reshaped opinion of him. The tall one dumped her tea in the sink and charged from the room.

Saul returned to his desk clutching at his throat. Maybe he should see a doctor. Maybe he needed drugs. He put his head down on his desk just before an authoritarian voice spoke. "Thank you for your hard work," the voice said, and Saul catapulted upright to find the new VP, the one charged with chopping their department down to profitable size, standing at his doorway with a butcher's smile.

Saul drank that night with two friends, Javier and Beckett. Both were transplants to Los Angeles who ignored the televisions featuring brawny fellows sprinting across fields and preferred to discuss the politics of the Middle East. Saul found that their diction level skyrocketed in proportion to the amount of beer consumed, as if alcohol exposed their true intelligence. But Saul had a strict two-beer limit. He'd had a bad experience in the Peace Corps while celebrating the completion of a well in Cote d'Ivoire and had not gotten drunk since.

During Saul's fourth beer, Beckett was telling a joke about his new girlfriend, a vegan seamstress, meeting his younger sister, a punk-rocker working at a charcuterie. Right at the punch line about rock stars eating vegans, Saul began shouting. He muffled it by sticking his face into his pint.

"Easy, Mr. Alcoholic. It's not the beer's fault," Beckett said.

"A wise man once said, 'Speak softly to beer. It will speak softly back,'" Javier said.

Saul wiped away the ring of foam around his mouth. Both Javier and Beckett were smiling, which meant they must not have heard what he yelled. "I don't feel well," he said.

"Well, Mr. Bantamweight, that's because you broke your two-beer limit," Beckett said. "Brutal day at the lie factory?"

"You know the antidote for drinking too much beer? Beer." Javier flagged the waitress.

Javier had a sister with autism, so perhaps he would be sympathetic to Saul's new malady. Neither of them were religious—Javier was not anything, and Beckett was a fully recovered Catholic who even called yogic ohms bullshit. That was partly why Saul got along with them so well.

So Saul told them about the shouting. When he finished he studied their faces, afraid of what he might find. Would they be able to tolerate him? Could he allow himself to foul up their social outings? Maybe it was better if he isolated himself rather than if they cut him from their lives. Of course, he was doing it again, the preemptive de-friending. This was why he broke up with every girlfriend before they could break up with him. This was why he kept his family distant, like a boxer with an extended arm. Gwen had pointed this out to him, citing as evidence the way he distanced himself from her as she wasted away, and he hated to admit she had been right.

Beckett tapped his glass twice with a fork. "I hear there's a lot of money in street preaching."

"That guy on Third Street could use a strong voice like yours," Javier said. "You could dress up in a superhero sidekick costume."

"You would wield a Bible. But a smaller one than the street preacher," Beckett said.

"Your Bible would have to be smaller. Sidekick rule. But it could be in a holster. And you could wear a cape."

"A smaller cape."

Saul fingered his fork, pressing the outer tine hard into his skin. He held it until the pink of his thumb faded to plaster.

"Really?" said Beckett.

"*Really?*" said Javier.

They both leaned back in disbelief. The list of advice began, such as visit a doctor, shrink, or voodoo priest. His friends batted about possibilities like PTSD from an unknown trauma and hypnotism from a nemesis in his office. During their speculating, the waitress sidled up. It was their usual waitress, for which they often left a large tip because she was shy and attractive. She stood in her normal place two steps back from the table.

"Can I get anyone another beer?"

"Go And Sin No More!"

It burst out with such speed he could not muffle it. There was no ambiguity, no chance of humor or irony. The waitress stepped back, frightened.

Saul saw surprise seize his friends' faces. Beckett's mouth expanded like a smoke ring and Javier's eyebrows arched. In a moment they would apologize. Or bark forced laughter, playing it off. Or joke that Saul was cut off. The shy waitress would recover. Saul would act penitent or drunk. And yet, however they smoothed over the awkward incident, Saul suspected the worst: that they would not stay friends with someone who had religious Tourettes.

The following day, Debra knocked on his cubicle wall. This was unexpected because there was not a door. It was also unexpected because he rarely talked to Debra, who handled accounting. Debra had the body type that people mocked as prototypically American, with flesh bulging around her hips and thighs, but he thought she liked him because last week he had gently steered a workplace conversation about obesity to a less controversial pasture.

"Saul, I just wanted to say thank you."

"Thank you for what?"

"For what you said on Wednesday."

Saul didn't remember speaking to Debra on Wednesday. As far as speaking in general on Wednesday, only one phrase stood out.

"About Jesus," Debra said.

"That was a complete accident—"

"Because you don't know this," Debra said. "Actually, no one knows this. On Wednesday morning I received a call that my father had had a heart attack, a second one, and it didn't look good. That's why I didn't come in until the next day, but just as I was feeling devastated, you said what you did, and I heard it while passing by the door, and it was a bolt from heaven. You said it right to me, even if you didn't know it. And my father was a very religious man and he was always disappointed that I wasn't faithful, so you reminded me what I needed to do. On Thursday night I went to the mid-week service at my old church with my mother, and we cried and prayed together, and even though it was one of the saddest nights of my life it was also one of the most beautiful. So I just wanted to thank you."

Saul regretted the delicacy of the situation. He wanted to issue an outright denial, but didn't want to wound her. "I'm glad that you feel united with God and your father," he said slowly. "But you overhearing that phrase was probably just a coincidence."

"There are no coincidences."

"I don't want to be mean. But maybe consider this might be exhibit A?"

"All things work together for good, Saul. You should know that."

"Well, it's true that many people want that to be true, and even I sometimes wish that was true. Still, I guess, I should say, well, forget it—"

"No, what?"

"I'm sorry for your father. I know what that's like, to be scared of losing... It's... I will... I will *hope* for him."

After Debra left, Saul thought how he'd been more scared of losing his sister than his sister was of losing herself. She had been uncharacteristically upbeat during her last months, optimistic that the chemotherapy and radiation would work a miracle. Even when she didn't mention religion, everything she said was colored with it. That lisp of hers, which he had always found endearing, ever since he beat up Beau Frankey in sixth grade for making fun of it, now grated on him—the way she pronounced "blessed" as "blethed." He should have visited her more often. During the last weeks he even avoided his parents. And he hated himself for it. Even though he knew it wasn't right, he couldn't stop himself.

Saul put his hands on the back of his head and dipped his forehead against the cool slab of his desk, bumping until it started to hurt. His head remained on his desk until the VP swung by and asked Saul to come with him. In the office of the VP, decorated in tasteful but formulaic décor, Saul sat in a chair, which was set a foot below the height of the VP's chair and could not, though he jiggled the lever twice, be raised. There was a second person in the office, a Human Resource guy in the corner, who reminded Saul of a rodent and who would not say a word.

"A valuable member of our team," the VP said with good cheer.

"Me?"

"I thank you for your time! People like you made our company. Look at this graph. This is your productivity, judged by blue, yellow, and red stripes. Your stripes were killing it. The last six months, though, they've leveled off."

"Which means I'm as effective as always, right?"

"Sometimes, putting your head down on your desk means you're trying to think up the next great PR campaign. I understand that. Innovation is important!"

"That really was an exception," Saul said.

"But there is this little, tiny, miniscule problem." The VP pinched his fingers together. "It's about you evangelizing at the workplace."

"What? No. Okay, maybe, once, kind of. But it was an accident."

"I get it," the VP said. "Between you and me," and he leaned forward and descended to a whisper, "I'm a man of faith, too. God, if he exists, should be advertised. But trying to convince fellow employees to change their religious beliefs by shouting at them? That might be the "H" word. *Harassment.*" The HR mute nodded.

"Listen. What happened was a rare, rare exception. I mistakenly said the wrong thing. It will not happen again."

"Whew. That was exactly the attitude I was looking for. I am so glad you're so accommodating."

"Thank you for understanding," Saul said.

"And of course we'll put you on unpaid leave while we examine the evidence."

"What?"

"It might take a while."

The HR mute nodded to confirm.

"There are only two women to talk to!"

"That's beside the point. Because I'm looking out for you, it might be in your best interest to find another job. You don't have to. You can fight this. But it will take a long time to sort out." The VP put on an expression of sympathetic condemnation.

While carrying a trash bag of desk items to his car, Saul wished that he had fought harder against the VP. He had no savings and refused to move back in with his parents. But he also felt, according to some mysterious math of the universe, that this was a punishment for his outbursts.

Saul drank alone at a bar but this time held himself to his two-beer limit. He started to call Javier twice but stopped. He didn't want to drag Javier or Beckett into this mess, especially if he started shouting again. Finally, he texted them both. Neither responded, and Saul sensed the silence was intentional. So he called the one person who would never pick up.

The phone rang five times before going to Gwen's voicemail. He felt thankful that some glitch had preserved her message, and listened to her lisping instructions about being brief yet thorough. On the first and second call, after the cheery finale of "God Bless," he hung up. On the third call he began to talk. He spoke of their mother dyeing her hair the color of unfired pottery before switching to the color of dried seaweed, which Saul found a strange way to process grief. He told her that their father had been making hefty, erratic contributions to charities like *Save the Butterfly Habitats* and *Man's Best Friend Adoption Agency*, and other odd foundations that protected the vulnerable. He told her that Scruffy had passed away under the table, probably out of loneliness. And he told her not to worry about him—it wasn't as though he had begun shouting things uncontrollably, of course not.

En route to his apartment, only five blocks away, he encountered a production crew shooting a movie. Given the size of the catered banquet and the number of hard-shell cases, it must have been a major studio. After he heard the words "Quiet on set," a horrific premonition began to grow. It was too late. As the actors began to recite their lines, he felt the carbonated words bubbling up from his gut and he began shouting in a tremendously loud voice: "Jesus Is The Light Of The World And He Came To Save

You From Your Sins Repent Now So He Will Have Mercy On Your Hell Bent Souls—" His hand muffled but did not quell the propaganda, so the director yelled cut, and the actors stopped and thirty-odd crewmembers looked at him with disgust. As if propelled by the surge of anger, a security guard and the assistant director rushed over.

"This is a fucking moral film," the A.D. said. "The claims online are lies. Lies!"

"Protest is legal," the security guard said to the A.D., talking around an electric cigarette. "Can't move him. But I can tell him that he's being a prick. Prick," he said to Saul.

"Why don't you move to a different city," the A.D. said. "Or go protest snuff films."

"Crazy fundamentalist," the guard said. The red light on his e-cigarette glowed reproachfully.

The two men waited for Saul's response. Behind them the entire crew waited. Saul read in their eyes the judgments that he had passed against others—that he was dogmatic, extremist, rabble-rousing, intolerant, liable to act violently against abortion doctors, to blindly vote for conservative politicians, and to demand schools teach only creationism. There was no way to defend himself, so he fled. He ran for two blocks before he grabbed a light pole to support his crumpling legs. He had become the person he had always despised.

On Saturday, Saul drove south to Orange County, a place which no longer had any orange groves. He was heading nowhere yet hoping that the nowhere would lead him somewhere. He took freeways and exited onto side streets. He saw hard hats laying pipe, a geysering fire hydrant, and medievally walled-off communities.

In the afternoon he came across a march. Two blocks of people waving signs. The signs were eclectic, none politicized by pro-life or pro-marriage, yet all religious, promising a future in heaven and rewards for good deeds. It was as if they were marching not for an agenda, but for the broader idea of faith.

Saul parked and followed them out of curiosity. At first he didn't embed himself in their ranks, but to cross a major street the police had erected a barricade that funneled all the marchers together. Saul found himself surrounded by the chanting crowd. A woman with red hair and a child on her hip pressed a sign into his hands, and though at first he held it at a halfhearted diagonal, he eventually raised it upright. It said, in a spooky coincidence, "God Will Save You."

Soon the marchers reached a large park filled with people, and on a stage a longhaired guitarist and two drummers played praise music. Saul did not want to join this religious riot but his fellow marchers left him no option. He was hustled into the main group. He'd hated crowds, ever since he'd encountered a rough mob in Nairobi, and stood with his arms close to his sides. In front of him stood a man with a child on his shoulders, the child blowing a whistle that sporadically matched the beat. To his right, a man skipped laterally, bumping a tambourine. To his left three teenage girls held hands and swayed with closed eyes, their mouths caressing the lyrics. Even though he didn't want to be here, he knew these were Gwen's type of people. Just by being here he felt closer to her.

At first he thought pickpocket—a hand glanced across his wrist. But the hand grabbed his wrist, not his wallet, and pressed a small palm against his. The hand belonged to one of the teenage girls, who had not even opened her eyes. He shivered in embarrassment—it was odd to hold the hand of such a young girl—but soon felt the pleasure of a physical link to another human being. He had not held hands since his sister's in the hospital, and he focused on how his skin felt calloused against the girl's soft flesh, and how a film of sweat developed between their palms. He even found himself starting to sway in tandem.

As the band provided a threshold of noise, an Indian man paced across the stage, urging people to sacrifice their throats to the living God. People shouted with heads thrown back and arms raised. As they continued, Saul remained silent. He felt disappointed that during the only acceptable time to shout, his malady did not visit him.

But the feeling rose. It wasn't like other times, like the premonition before vomiting. This was a feeling of delight, like the rising anticipation before an orgasm. He began to shout phrases in a loud voice, fast as an auctioneer: "You Are The Alpha And Omega And Able To Save Us So Lord Jesus Christ Have Mercy On Those Who Call On The Name Of The Lord Jesus Christ And Wish To Be Saved Even Those Sinners Headed For Damnation Lord Jesus Christ Who Died On That Cross And Rose Again Please Grant Us Your Power And Glory And Dominion Forever And Ever..." He couldn't stop, even after the whistle-blowing child and father and teenage girls and tambourine man laid hands on him. He shouted for minutes, with his legs flexed and the tendons in his neck standing out like piano strings. Surprisingly, as he listened to his own voice, he heard himself lisping.

The words stopped. Saul was sweaty and exhausted, like a long fever had broken. He took stock of those surrounding him and was reminded that these people, despite their kind intentions, were so estranged from his world. One wore a false-dichotomy T-shirt—"Jesus VS. Satan: Who Will You Serve?" Another's wrist bracelet promoted the Christian female rappers, "Em & Em." This march had thrown him into a place he could not belong.

He brushed the hands off his body and tried to leave the park, pressing through the dense crowd. He thought he was backtracking to his street, but lost his bearings. The crowd seemed labyrinthine. When he stood on his toes to gain a line of sight, he saw the bodies of additional devotees flocking to the fringes, extending the circle's range to the faintest flickers of the floodlights. His claustrophobia kicked in, making his hands tremble.

He saw Gwen. Auburn hair in a bob, avian-thin shoulders, the precise slope of nose and cut of chin. She was only thirty feet away. It could not be Gwen and yet it was. He called her name and his voice cracked midway. The crowds shifted and he lost his line of sight, so he began to bully through bodies. Through the gaps in the crowd he caught glimpses of her hair and he pressed on, sending people staggering from his passage. He felt if he did not find her all would be lost. But when he reached the spot, he could not find her. He had gone the appropriate distance and no one could have escaped his scrutiny, but he was alone in the crowd. He felt tricked. The music assaulted his ears. His legs felt weak, so weak that they folded beneath him until he sat cross-legged in the exact spot where she had stood.

A dark forest of legs surrounded him. Above him were gray torsos, swaying in time to the beat, and above that the heads of the multitudes. Arms jutted above the heads, and above their fingertips the massive wings of trees stretched over the gathering. Finally, in a space between branches, he saw the grand, wise sky, with stars leaking light, and for the first time it looked close enough for him to touch.

The City of God and the City of Man

They called me Inspector. Which was what I did, but such a modest term downplayed my role. My true occupation was saving people. Let me be clear: I was not a mere inspector of restaurants. Alphabeters—my term for them, since wherever they slouched they left a letter grade behind—were chained to culinary establishments, while I hunted for health code violations across the spread of the business world. Now this might sound dull to a tin-eared bore, but as I've proven to everyone at parties, it can be thrilling. The filth of an FA-141 bathroom violation, an outbreak of mold at Christmas trees lots, a chemical leak that scars a floor radioactive green— all these stories riveted the listeners. And I have power as well. I can shut a business down, if the violation warrants it. I have that kind of authority.

The call came as I left for work. As my phone vibrated, I kissed Napoleon goodbye on her cheeks three times, French style, because of her French bulldog pedigree. She was dying on me, and every day I was afraid of her stilled form when I returned. I held the door to a crack and gazed at her one pleading eye.

"I can't stay home. I can't. I'm sorry." She acknowledged my apology with a bark.

The number had a 213 area code: Los Angeles. I had many numbers in my phone, but no one who knew me ever called.

"Mr. Cade Newbigin? I wish to report a violation."

"You should be calling the hotline," I said.

"The Holy Land has a secret."

"I don't think they're keeping the resurrection thing a secret."

"They have violations."

I'd inspected the Holy Land last year when it opened in Fullerton. It was a religious theme park, funded by billionaire brothers with rhyming names, and they appeared to believe that cleanliness was next to godliness.

"Could you be more specific?"

The caller very specifically hung up on me.

I drove to work in Anaheim, arriving six minutes early. As I walked to my office I nodded at colleagues, but several, including Preston Griffin, ignored me.

In my office I started playing Gem Tower Defense. I'd played daily for six years, twice placing on the High Score list by reaching level 116, which took about seven hours. I found it soothing to watch my gems erode the life force of the little men filing through my maze. It felt like a drug. If I ever reached level 130, I imagined a message would appear, solving a mystery of the universe or revealing a secret about myself.

About two hours into the morning I died on level forty-four, the one where the flying birds double their speed, so I decided to visit the Holy Land. Since protocol demanded advance notice, I called the park and said I was coming in an hour.

The theme park had been built in Fullerton's West Coyote Hills, a site formerly owned by Chevron, who'd humped it dry of oil and sold it to avoid EPA-mandated cleanups. It was far from the 5 and 91, but visitors probably considered the long commute on side streets as a pilgrimage.

A woman was waiting for me at the gates of the walled city, next to three teens dressed like Roman soldiers, wearing plastic armor and clutching spears like joysticks.

"Mr. Newbigin, I presume," she said, extending her hand. She had a lazy eye, so I wasn't sure where to look, but I was still attracted to her. "Ella Knight."

"Mrs. Knight, thank you for meeting me on such short notice."

"*Miss* Knight," she said. "And why this inspection today?"

I was relieved to hear about the Miss. "My office got an anonymous tip about public health conditions at your park."

Miss Knight rolled her good eye. "The Humanist Park," she said bitterly.

"Excuse me?"

"An anonymous tip? A 213 area code? They've been trying to sabotage us since we opened."

"If this was sabotage, that is illegal and unfortunate. But I will still need to see the park."

"Fine," she said in an un-fine voice. She grabbed my elbow and pulled me out of the way of an Egyptian pharaoh riding a "chariot"—a Segway with red and white Styrofoam modifications. I was happy to be pulled anywhere by her.

She started to guide me through the crowds of tourists. "These are hollow plaster," she said in a brisk, flat tone, pointing at the manikins depicting Biblical scenes—the manger, woman at the well, soldiers casting lots. "Same for the stations of the cross."

Fourteen Christs with crosshatched backs and crowns of thorns crawled through the Stations of the Cross: gross, but not unsanitary. I scribbled in my notebook, determined to do a good and rigorous job, but feeling Miss Knight's eyes on my pen.

From a beige hill in the park center, a thirty-foot statue of Jesus began to rise, accompanied by the Hallelujah chorus. It was so loud she leaned into me and shouted in my ear. "Here, Jesus rises from the dead every half hour." From her raised eyebrows, she appeared to find this an improvement over the traditional story.

"Bathroom?" I asked. As she led the way, an Easter parade ambushed us. A Jesus actor rode a donkey through braced-teeth girls fanning him with palm branches and shrieking at pop-star-worship levels. I had to scurry out of the way to avoid being trampled, which summed up my experience with religion. For reasons I didn't understand, I kept putting myself in the way of religion, only to run away at the last moment. Miss Knight didn't even glance at the Jesus, just stayed very on-task.

Past the falafel and hummus stand I walked into the men's bathroom and found Miss Knight had followed me inside.

"If this is official business," she said.

"Could you please wait outside?" I said. I wasn't ready for that level of intimacy yet.

Once she left, I scanned it. Nothing near an FA-141 violation. Some scanty caulking. A leak, plops echoing in the tile. Since a Pharisee decorated each urinal and a disciple hung above each sink, I pissed in Gamaliel and washed my hands in Peter, then rejoined Miss Knight, who glanced at my notebook as if wishing she could read it before shredding it.

At the carousel, which played "Onward Christian Soldiers" as young visitors rode elephants, lions, serpents, and golden calves, she asked me: "Are you a believer, Mr. Newbigin?"

I pretend-coughed into the crook of my elbow. Two teenage passengers hung off their snake and ass to fight with each other, in yet another case of religious violence. "I don't think it's proper for us to discuss personal matters."

"True, religion is never proper to talk about. It'd be easier for us to talk about sex or money than to talk about religion. But in this case, your personal beliefs matter, don't they?"

The operator had stopped the carousel because of the fight between the teenagers, which turned out to be a play fight between friends, but I was more interested in the life beneath the carousel. I skipped rocks beneath until a blur streaked from the undercarriage and sought refuge in a nearby drain. A rat! I glanced back at Miss Knight, who had blanched. I wrote very authoritatively in my notebook.

"How about we visit The Last Supper?" she asked in a small voice, and led me to a dark theater, where the show was already in progress. Stage lights illuminated twelve animatronic figures behind a table. A voice-over dramatized the scene, with the Jesus figure jawing his lines. The twelve apostles shuddered through predestined moves: necks rotated, arms jerked, torsos tilted, each piece quivering in place at its designated station. I guessed Miss Knight had taken me here hoping I wouldn't be able to notice anything in the dark, but as a veteran health inspector I knew dark places often had violations.

After the show ended, Miss Knight and I went to the gloom behind the stage. On the cock bulge of the disciple on the end I saw graffiti of a wide-eyed child with a balloon. Quite an accusation against the church, given the scandals of recent years. But that was minor compared to the floor. My shoes stepped into a sticky muck. The tar-like substance oozed from near the graffitied apostle, smelling of sulfur. It reminded me of the black stool Napoleon shat out just before I learned he had colon cancer.

"What is it?" Miss Knight asked. She couldn't see the tar in the dark. Then the squeaking began. Just behind her head, the animatronic figures were all still except for one: the Jesus, squeakily swiveling his head. The Jesus continued to turn his head until it was completely backwards, and the menacing black oval burned through me.

I found no other violations. She promised to get a mechanic on The Last Supper pronto, and though I could cite them on a CH-322—a hazardous chemical spill—I didn't consider

John Matthew Fox

that necessary. I did tell Miss Knight I'd have to cite them on the rat infestation, and she promised to hire an exterminator. I shook hands with her before I left, focusing on her good eye.

On the drive from Fullerton to Anaheim, I thought about her believer question. The answer was complicated. For instance.

I had a strange habit. Some Sundays chose me at random. On those mornings a force other than myself decided that I would go to a service, and prepared me until I sat in the car all dressed up and there was nothing left for me to do other than sleepily follow the commands of my navigation system. When I arrived, I never entered the chapel/auditorium/ warehouse. I sat outside, catching strains of the music. I stayed until the service ended and the building flushed people out, and I scrutinized them, memorizing their gestures, their laughter, their sadness, and trying to detect how they'd changed between their entrance and exit. Then I drove away camouflaged by the grand exodus. I never went back to a place. When I returned to my driveway, I often had a feeling like I'd sleepwalked and committed some terrifying deed that I could remember only in spurts and shadows.

I didn't believe in God. I didn't hold to any tenets of faith— like the afterlife, reincarnation, angels, or mitzvahs. I didn't pledge allegiance to any theology or dogmas. I didn't have religious friends. As a teen I once asked my mother, a holiday Presbyterian, whether I should be religious, and she said, "Cade, you have to find your own path." Which seemed nice and open-minded, but it wasn't, because my path left me confused.

Back at the office I found a delivery on my desk so large it had displaced my French bulldog mugs. A basket filled with Ghirardelli truffles, beige wafers, tins of peanut brittle, and Guatemalan coffee beans. No letter identified the sender, though I guessed the Humanist Park. I didn't drink coffee, but if I gave the beans to Preston I might earn the right to be acknowledged—and maybe even hear my name—when I arrived in the morning.

I called my inspector friend in Los Angeles to inquire about the Humanist Park. We inspectors are quite chummy. Nobody can understand the stress of the job like another inspector, and when I attended the annual conference there was nothing better than to sit at the bar and swap stories. Everyone always listened raptly to mine; at conferences I set my storytelling ability to stun.

"Who?" my friend asked twice, after I'd repeated my name. I wasn't the type to insinuate, but he might have been drinking on the job.

"Right, right," he said. "What can I do you for?"

As soon as I mentioned the Humanist Park he interrupted me.

"Funny about your call," he said. "An anonymous rang me ten minutes ago reporting some violations there."

"Orange County area code?" I asked.

"Spot on," he said.

"Even though I think this is a case of revenge, you still should investigate," I said.

"No can do," he said. "Conflict of interest. Me and the manager, we acted together back in the day. Did waiters and bellhops in TV pilots that never got picked up. And my Santa Monica colleague is vacationing in Buenos Aires. Think you can handle it?"

I thought of the honor of leaving my jurisdiction to preside over an investigation in a neighboring county. Even my fellow workers in Anaheim would respect me for handling such a prestigious assignment. Of course I accepted.

I loved the sound when I fitted my key in the lock: an impatient bark, a scrabbling of toenails at the door. Every day I feared the door would be silent, and every day my fears were unfounded. Napoleon was a sausage of loose skin and love. I kissed her cheeks, alternating between right and left, French-style. I let her run around the back yard until dinner. She ate her wheat-free, organic-beef dog food, and I microwaved a frozen meal for myself.

Napoleon sat in my lap while I played Gem Tower Defense. Eventually, only the screen and myself existed. It was a private congress between my brain and a machine. I could feel the drip of it back in my throat, like a cold that wouldn't go away. I even forgot about Napoleon, until she whined to go outside. It was very different from what I felt on those Sunday mornings.

Every Sunday when I waited in my car during the services, I hoped to hear the music. It felt deliciously illicit to eavesdrop on worship, because it was so intimate and yet not my own, like hearing my neighbors moan and thump through sex. Sometimes during the service I cracked open my door and dipped a foot onto the asphalt. It felt sneaky, like I was stealing. After each service I fantasized about getting out of my car and walking among the herds of the departing, keeping my sights straight but brushing against an outcropping of sleeve, the fringe of a dress, the chapped skin of an elbow. But I never did.

In Gem Tower Defense I died on level one hundred at two a.m., and I was glad because my joy had vanished thirty levels ago and I'd kept playing only out of duty. When I put Napoleon to bed, I whispered in her ear, "Live, live. I love you." She nuzzled into the blanket and licked my cheeks on both sides. Imitating me! But as I went to bed, I thought that even my desire for her was selfish—I wanted her to live because I didn't want to be alone.

The Humanist Park was just north of downtown Los Angeles, in Silver Lake. The parking attendants wore Swiss-inspired outfits, with suspenders and short shorts. I reminded myself that I was not doing this investigation as a favor for Miss Knight.

The manager, Wilfred Mange, was waiting for me outside the marble entrance arch. He was a large man, both overweight and big-framed, with a goatee that bristled like a sea urchin. I suspected he played base in a cover band.

"Welcome to the land of enlightenment," he said, and we walked through the arch.

"Do you know about the Holy Land?" I asked.

"What an awful situation," Wilfred said. "The Palestinians deserve their own state. Joking! Of course Mrs. Knight sent you here. Do you know she hired actors in bathrobes to hand out pamphlets for the Holy Land at our park entrance? And they weren't even clean bathrobes or good actors!"

"I believe it's *Miss* Knight," I said.

Wilfred glanced at me sidelong. "You'll remain impartial in this investigation, won't you Mr. Newbigin?"

We crossed the Bridge of Analytic Thought, adorned with busts of Kant and Spinoza and Nietzsche, and I saw the Baptism of Reason log ride, where logs floated down a water canal. Over the tops of nearby buildings a huge spire swayed in the breeze, and the upper loops of a roller coaster spiraled. The shrieks of the riders crescendoed and died. If the track snapped and the passengers plunged to their deaths, I wondered how the humanists would comfort the relatives.

"I'd like to check the log ride for mold, then have colleagues of mine test that spire."

"The spire's nickname is Big Johnson," Wilfred said. "Get it? Get it? But trust me, whatever Knight told you was wrong."

"It was an anonymous report."

"There's anonymous and then there's anonymous."

"You also engaged in a little bit of anonymous reporting, did you not?"

Wilfred coughed twice. "Let me catch you a log."

I am not the type to ride carnival rides, but for the sake of my professional reputation, I stepped into the log Wilfred arranged for me. The first room showed philosophers levitating when a light bulb blinked on over their head. My log slid down an incline, nearing a castle where windows and drawbridges sprung open to reveal lab coats pouring from beaker to beaker and spectacled women of color solving math problems on chalkboards. Next, my log rattled over a series of humps to simulate rapids and approached a gigantic see-through head, with an electrical board for a brain. Here I spotted suspicious locations with fuzzy growth. At the end of the ride, the log climbed a long ramp and fell down a steep slope, where I was not sprinkled but immersed by a giant wave.

"You got soaked!" Wilfred said. "What a surprise!" He went into the conveniently located gift shop and fetched me a T-shirt that said, "Science: It Works, Bitches!" and sweatpants that said across the bum, "Logic > Faith."

When I came back from changing, he had some hot fries ready for me.

"Freethinker fries!" he said. "The antidote to repressed thinking *and* to repressed waistlines." He patted his expansive belly and laughed. He mowed through the majority of the fries, while I glanced at the passersby. None of them were smiling, but I still felt more comfortable here. In the Holy Land I always worried that someone would expose me, as if they had a device scanning the park for unbelievers and would send evangelists to intercept me. But here, I could believe anything as long as it was science-friendly and Enlightenment-based and limited to the material universe.

"Tell me this," Wilfred Mange said, with a mouth full of fries. "Do you have a crush on her? Is that why you're harassing us? Oh my god, you do! You blush like a sunset."

"Do not insinuate I am being anything less than professional, or I will write you up for every violation in this park."

"Mr. Newbigin. Think about your last relationship."

"Let's not—"

"Just think."

I thought about my last date. It had been years ago. After a long time of trying, I gave up on anything as advanced as a relationship. But Napoleon kept me company, at least. And Gem Tower Defense kept me occupied. With both of them I didn't have to feel so lonely.

"The Holy Land is like a girlfriend you didn't actually date but who still insisted on breaking up with you and stalking you. A relationship from hell. The Humanist Park would get away from her if we could but we can't. We have to live with her. But you have the power to make this less painful. You can choose who you want to support, and who you want to punish. Think about our two parks and what they stand for. You want to be on the right side of history, correct? Choose the right relationship. You can do it."

The following day, as I did copious amounts of paperwork in my office, Miss Ella Knight knocked at my door. I stood up so abruptly I had to steady myself on the desk.

"Sit, sit," she said, and sat herself.

Her good eye surveyed my office, which now seemed shabby. A single poster from a nondescript beach hung on the wall, sandwiched between my official certifications.

"If you have ears to hear, hear this," she said. "I have sacrificed my entire life for this park. I have put my career on the line, my savings on the line. Please don't let smooth talking saboteurs ruin it."

"I doubt it will come to ruin."

"Thank you." She placed a palm on my desk. "And I just wanted to assure you that we are handling the violations. We hired an exterminator for Noah's Carousel and have shut down The Last Supper to retrofit the engine."

"I'm glad to hear that," I said. Preston Griffin passed by, double-taking when he glimpsed the shock of blonde hair. I hoped he felt jealous.

"I also heard you inspected our competitor?" She smiled artificially.

"I can't comment on ongoing investigations."

"If you do need to shut them down, I would not be opposed." She forced a laugh.

"I will perform my job, Miss Knight."

"I can read people." She crimped her finger at me. "And I can tell you're a great worker. You're an honorable man. You are not the type to be swayed by bribes." She looked at the basket in the corner. I'd eaten half of it already.

I told myself to resist her charm, and focused on her bad eye. "Are you trying to sabotage the humanist park?" I asked. "Because Wilfred Mange—"

"Imagine if the world was filled with people like Wilfred," she said. "We would lack any sensitivity, any grasp of grace. The world would outlaw all beliefs that couldn't be verified in a lab."

She was beautiful when passionate, and I wanted to retain that image of her. I stood and gestured at the door, and she left graciously. If all this washed out well, I would take a night off Gem Tower and ask her to dinner. If I could stomach a night away from the game.

Two hours later, in the middle of a Gem Tower Defense game, my phone rang. Wilfred Mange started talking before I'd gotten the receiver to my ear. "Do not let Miss Knight persuade you," he said. "You should be shutting down the Holy Land without delay. Not only because of health violations, but because of mental violations. For how they are indoctrinating small children."

"I'm pretty sure another department handles mental abuse," I said.

"Listen to me," he said. "Choose the city of man over the city of God."

"Wilfred, how's the mold in your log ride?"

Silence. I hung up on him and paced my office for almost an hour before deciding to compose an email to both of them:

I am not shutting down either of your parks, although maybe I should shut down both. But it is impossible to close one and not the other, as your violations are equal in severity. Although the multiple violations at both parks warrant immediate attention, I found nothing that cannot be redressed. I would please ask you to stop using this office as a battleground between your respective businesses/ideologies, and remind you that hatred-motivated reporting of violations against a competing business could be grounds for fines and/or legal action.

Preston poked his head in my door. "Cade! Thanks for the coffee." He was gone before I could respond. Still, I basked in that brief glow of attention.

On my drive home I remembered the time last year when I'd staked out a religious service. I'd seen an online advertisement about a baptism ceremony at the Santa Ana River, and although I'd tried to forget it, the place and time had wedged itself in my memory. So I found myself on the freeway that Sunday. The car parked itself far from other cars and a hill padded with leaves gave way before me and a granite boulder over the crest presented itself for a seat. Using some old binoculars, I looked through the bar code of tree trunks. Down by the river people milled. I told myself that the water was probably polluted, and that the weekend hordes changed the ratio of water and urine to 1:1, but as I watched, my cynicism fell away like scales.

The pastor gestured from the shallows, people in white robes filed into the spangled river, and one by one they were dunked and rose again. Oh, the chance to start over! The chance to be new! The power of it swept up the hill, tingling the soles of my feet. The cycle continued, person after person. When bodies sprung from the water, the light flashed from them, as if they'd been dipped in metal and reflected a newfound brightness, and the lenses of my binoculars flushed white, and after the color and shapes surged back, the final glittering drops fell from their hair and arms and the cloth clung to their bodies so tightly it seemed like they were wearing nothing at all.

At my house there were no sounds when I put my key in the lock, and that jolted my heart. I tore through every room yelling Napoleon's name. I found her in front of the drier, still as death, but in the shadows I noticed the stub of a tail waving like an abbreviated flag. Oh, that stubborn tail! She lacked the strength to lift her head. I cradled and kissed her until my lips burned from her bristles. With my back against the drier I waited in the darkness for a miracle, but knew none would come. She couldn't have much time left. Maybe hours. I considered visiting the vet and sending her out on a pillow of drugs, but I was no more capable of that than euthanizing my parents.

So we played Gem Tower Defense. I wanted to share it with her one last time. As I picked my gems and built my maze, I held her against my chest and timed my breath so we inhaled and exhaled at the same time. If she died I wanted to die, too.

In the game I got extraordinarily lucky. I got five double diamonds and loads of Dark Emerald and Gold towers. The game went so well that I reached level 117! A new record! Now I had a new goal: to reach level 130. I'd always imagined that level would reveal something to me. Drunk on the lateness of the hour, I half imagined it would even save Napoleon.

It was a miracle I didn't die on level 120, 124, or 128. An hour later I reached level 130 and sat back like I'd reached the vista of a previously unexplored continent. I lifted Napoleon up and showed her the screen, awaiting a revelation. But it was still the same game, still the same men winding through the maze. The same screen I'd stared at for the last eight hours, the same screen for the last six years. I suddenly hated it. My stomach rolled sour and I felt like strangling myself. On level 131 I committed suicide by removing crucial stones.

"Why did we play this so much?" I asked Napoleon. Her eyes were glassy. I shut my laptop and the room sunk into darkness. The curtains lit up with the faint glow from the streetlamp. It would be dawn in a few hours, with the sun burning through the curtains and searing the walls, but right now the light seemed so far away.

I needed to be a better Inspector. I needed to inspect the shape and bends of the universe, and the hidden currents inside the human heart, and the scaffolding up to the heavens. Parts of Napoleon's hair had been brushed in contradictory directions so I smoothed it. The room smelled like hot flesh. I had been too shallow, too shortsighted. I had not inspected enough of the world, or been curious enough, and already I felt old. Napoleon breathed shallowly in my arms. The end of her breath came in a rasp. All that mattered was her breath and my breath, her heartbeat and my heartbeat. God, I needed to be a better Inspector.

God's Guerrilla

Once I decided to go visit my daughter Catherine and the grandkids in Portland, not even the Devil himself could have stopped me. Driving up without speaking engagements seemed a waste of my talent, so I placed a few calls. I told one pastor I was doing a steeplechase up the coast, a bit of wordplay I found uproarious, but his humor was off as old cheese. "Randolf," he said, approaching my name like a wild animal, "I think you frightened a few of our high schoolers last time." I held the phone like a barbell and said, "Nothing wrong with a little fright!"

So that apostate turned me down, but I booked two others. My shtick dramatized stories from the holy battlefield. Closest I came to guns-and-bombs action was serving as a chaplain in the early years of the Vietnam war, but let me tell you, I've run the gauntlet: I've dealt the Word in eighteen languages, survived a poisonous snake bite, smuggled Bibles across hostile borders, outlasted three imprisonments (one solitary), and abetted two exorcisms. Technically I was retired, but there weren't any laggards in the army of God, only those taking a resting spell. So I rested up and did my duty.

My daughter loved surprises, so I didn't call beforehand. On Wednesday I put on the brown corduroy suit with thin wales and drove up Pacific Coast highway with all four windows down on Ehud, my battered Buick. Ehud had endured several assaults, including Halloween sabotages involving maple syrup and eggs because I gave out verses instead of candy for the pagan holiday, but it never stopped running.

Just after dusk, I arrived in Eureka and found my first church. The youth pastor sported cheeks with virginal fuzz. When we shook, I squeezed hard. He winced, but said, "Nice. In the flesh. God's Guerrilla." I put on the stoic look suitable for such a nickname, with a lowered chin and hard eyes. I'd been dubbed that in the seventies, after kamikaze trips smuggling Bibles through the Iron Curtain. I should have been shot, poisoned, or betrayed more times than Caesar and Mandela combined, but a halo of safety hovered on my crown. "You ready to have your world rocked?" He nodded as though I were promising him streets of gold.

In the church, the kids sprinted around a circle with bowling pins and beanbags. I wanted to join but they said no. I told them I was fast as Elijah, but that didn't sway them. Once the twenty-odd high schoolers were penned in the front rows, I related one of my earliest missionary adventures in Laos. We were floating down the Mekong. Mist garlanded the trees. Howler monkeys shrieked from the canopies. And then nothing. Not in the story nothing, but in my mind nothing. My mental slate had been squeegeed clean, even though I'd relayed this story thousands of times. The kids' faces went through stages—at first they believed I'd taken a dramatic pause, then they rustled into inattentiveness, then they started to doubt me. Hell's bells! I shifted to another story, then fumbled and failed to remember two. Since the message ended dreadfully short, I prayed for an eternity to stretch things out.

I fled to my motel. Since my memory had always been sharp as a whittling knife, I'd never needed to write anything down, but now I played scribe to my top-rate story, about how I used a blow dart competition to convince a penis-gourd aboriginal tribe in Indonesia that I bore the gospel truth. I could see every cheek and forehead piercing of the tribe leader, even though it happened forty years ago. Glory be! Hadn't lost it all.

That night, lying in bed, I conducted tests. Birthdate of Linda, my late wife, who could hum and whistle at the same time. Grandkids' birthdates. The defunct wedding anniversary of my daughter Catherine, who once ate only Skittles for a month until I force-fed her real food. Checkety check-check. It didn't make sense. I did fifty pushups every morning to fend off mental fog. I made every crossword puzzle my bondservant.

Before I fell asleep, I decided to call my daughter. We'd chat, but I wouldn't tell her I was coming. Surprises were best. The phone rang nine times but no answering machine picked up. I called again. When Catherine answered, she launched a volley of hellos, but I just kept silent. Finally, I chuckled. "I can hear you laugh," she said. And then she added a word entirely inappropriate for redeemed ears. Shameful, so shameful. I slammed the phone down. But thank heaven for forgiveness—I'd let it go by the time my cheek hit the pillow.

On the second leg of the drive, I wore my seersucker suit and followed the coast up to Oregon, cutting east along a two-lane logging road where several unredeemed drivers nearly sideswiped my beautiful Ehud. All the retirees drove slowly, so to counter them, I drove faster than normal, zipping between lanes, ignoring the honks, which helped me arrive at Catherine's house before dark.

As my daughter opened the door, her head retracted, turtle-like. "Pop."

I gave a faith-healer grin and held out my hands.

"Why are you here?" she asked.

"Catherine. You look more gorgeous than ever."

She eyed my suitcase. "You weren't planning on staying, were you?"

"What wonderful hospitality," I yelled, and swept in for a hug. "Where's the grandkids?" It was rhetorical. The deaf could hear their video games. I marched to the living room.

"Gramps," the eldest, Terrance, said. "How are you?" Since I last saw him all his bones had elongated but his skin and muscles hadn't kept up.

"I'm getting stronger and wiser," I said. "You?"

"I'm good."

"No," I said. "Good won't cut it. You're doing terrific. Repeat after me: terrific!"

He said it, but his body, slouched on the couch, belied it. "You look strong as the sons of Anak," I told him, squeezing his forearm. "Flex for me."

He reluctantly flexed. It looked more tendon-like than muscular, but I still grunted with appreciation. Three cuts ran parallel along the inner flesh of his bicep, too neat to be accidental. He asked who the sons of Anak were.

"Catherine!" I said. "You not teaching these kids their Old Testament history?" She crossed her arms.

"Race of giants," I told him, poking him in the nook of the collarbone as punishment. "Their famous descendant was Goliath. Heard of him?" He squirmed away.

"Granddaddy," Mirabelle said. She'd been working on a popsicle-stick cathedral, her hands sticky with glue. "Am I a daughter of A-nack?"

"No, no, no," I said. "You're descended from Eric Liddell, the runner and missionary."

"Granddaddy, listen to my memorization," she said. She started to recite verses from Philippians in a monotone, until after two chapters I suspected she wouldn't stop unless I cut in.

"Your mother had you too late in life," I said. "What a blessing you didn't turn out retarded!"

"Let me guess," Catherine said drily. "Now you're going to tell her one of your stories."

Normally I would have scooped Mirabelle into my lap and regaled her with a swashbuckling tale of missionary adventure, but I worried that as soon as I started to speak, the story would vanish and I'd sit there stupidly.

"What a pretty dress!" I told her. Then I hemmed and hawed while Catherine looked at me strangely. After a while I stopped and no one else spoke. I started to slip into the catatonic state that too many men my age fall into—bolted to their chairs, minds more porridge than cerebrum. My grandson leaned toward me, concerned. In his pupils I saw a reflection of my lifeless frame. I didn't want that to be his memory.

"Let's get ice cream!" I shouted.

Even though it was dinnertime, my heroic charm convinced Catherine to drive us to the Scoop Shack. The kids got bizarre flavors, so I complimented their courage and braved a raspberry and mint concoction. Catherine refused to eat one, even after I told her three times she wasn't getting fat. It was always so difficult to make her eat, and then she'd gorge herself. When Mirabelle didn't know how to get the last smears of ice cream, I demonstrated how to lick the cup. Catherine rolled her eyes. "Let's go out to dinner," I said.

"No," Catherine said. "Money's been in short supply."

"What? Dennis failed in that department, too?"

"Still going through legal."

I rattled off a list of invectives that would have seared the ears of innocent bystanders: Son of Apostasy. Prophet of Heresy. King of Reprobates. "Fine then," I said. "I'll pay."

Mirabelle cheered. Terrance looked at his mother.

"You don't have any money," she said.

"*Au contraire*," I said. I took out the honorarium and flapped the bills around.

Catherine wore the expression of someone who'd already given in. "Pop. If we go out, will you please behave yourself?"

"Will I behave myself? I'm the poster boy for godliness."

We went to a diner where all the waitresses wore poodle skirts, but trust me, I was around for the originals and they weren't nearly as risqué. I shielded my eyes as I ordered. "Pop," Catherine hissed.

When the food came, I offered to pray. The grandkids put their food down, as if unused to the tradition, and Catherine hurriedly volunteered, but I claimed the honor as head of the household. I stood in the booth, arms raised. "Yahweh: Bless this cow that has sacrificed its flesh for our sustenance. And bless the potatoes and wheat. Please curse the corporations that damage our pocketbooks and protect us from unhealthiness. Amen." Catherine's hands were welded to her face like horse blinders. Someone across the restaurant recognized a solid prayer when they heard one because they started clapping.

Halfway through the best burger of my life, my cell phone rang. It was the second pastor. "Randolf, I just wanted to see if you were still coming tomorrow."

"The four horsemen of the apocalypse couldn't stop me," I said. Then I remembered my problem and wanted to suck back all my words. But a vow was a vow, as binding as if we'd grabbed each other's inner thigh.

"Good," he said. "Because last time—"

"Oh, that'll never happen again." I hung up.

"Who was that?" Catherine asked.

"Can you drive me to Gresham on Saturday night?" I asked. "I need moral support."

"I can't. Terrance has his basketball game."

"Gramps, you should come," Terrance said.

"I would love to see that. Do you dunk? Can you throw it down like good ole Wilt?"

"Who's Wilt?"

"Chamberlain!"

"I'm close," he said.

"He can almost touch the rim," Catherine said.

"In our resurrection bodies, you'll be able to jump from half court and stuff it," I said.

Catherine used a napkin to wipe nothing off her face and motioned for the check even though we weren't finished eating.

"I would love a madeleine," I said, rubbing my belly. "No, a malt. We should get malts."

"We had ice cream before dinner," Catherine said.

Of the two malts we bought, I ended up drinking one and a half. Maybe calcium aided memory.

Back at the house, Terrance returned to his video game and Catherine herded Mirabelle away from the popsicle-stick cathedral and toward bed. Afterwards, I followed Catherine to the master bedroom, which was already cleansed of photographs of Dennis.

"How are you holding up since the great apostate left?" I asked.

"Why haven't you called?"

"I did call. Last night."

"That was you? I thought it was him again."

"Dennis doesn't talk? He just calls and hangs up?"

She reached for the alarm, tapping in an early time. Strange how skinny her arms had stayed. They hadn't grown since Malaysia. Also strange that I could remember the diameter of her arms and couldn't remember what I did there for a year and a half. I did remember this: When Catherine was young, she insisted that she couldn't fall asleep until I'd told her goodnight and read her a Bible story. Turned out she got insomnia pretty often. I just had too many souls to save from the roasts of hellfire. But I read often enough, I thought. When I could.

"Pop, are you all right?"

"Better than all right. Terrific." I came to attention and saluted. "Reporting for Hamilton family duty."

She folded her hands in her lap. "Because usually you're telling stories left and right but I didn't hear one from you all day."

The hammock under my left eye twitched. It was not the time. "I'm building suspense," I said. "Scarcity creates demand."

"Your head's still working fine, though?"

I snorted. "My noggin's a lockbox. Test me!"

"I don't want to test you, Pop."

"You have to. Pick a test."

She rubbed her eyes. "Fine, if I have to." She thought for a moment. "Why don't you name all the different schools I attended?"

"Perfect. Great test." I began slapping outstretched fingers with my index. "The boarding school for M.K.s in the Philippines. That one-room thing on the Ecuadorian coast led by that warty-faced woman. Didn't we homeschool you for six months? Twice? No, three times. The M.K. school in South Africa—rather segregated, but still good, right? The house in Kansas on our first furlough, and that school in Seattle on our second, and that basement in New Jersey on our third. See? Isn't that good?"

She stayed impossibly still.

"Don't be sore," I said. "Don't. It was for the Kingdom."

"I'm sure the Kingdom did quite well."

"But look how smart you are," I said. "And beautiful."

"Yes, look how beautiful Dennis found me."

"Forget him. His harlot's probably ugly."

"Ugly, no. Younger, yes. But Pop, you know the kids have missed you."

"I'm a stevedore on the heavenly docks! Busy, busy, busy!"

She didn't pause. "And if you ever find yourself sliding downhill in terms of health, you need to tell me. You can't live in that rundown shanty you call an apartment forever."

She took off her earrings and put them inside the jewelry box that used to be my wife's. From the back, with her hair curly and down, she looked like her mother, during the nightly ritual of taking off a dress and facing me with nothing but a slip and love.

On Friday, I donned my white linen suit, which made me look like Billy Graham. Catherine, gussied up in a gray pantsuit, blended fruit and raw eggs before slopping the red slush into glasses. Terrance staggered to the table and Mirabelle bounced like a caffeinated harpy. Catherine reminded Terrance he should practice basketball.

"Basketball?" I said. "I will make you my bondservant."

"Mom," he said. "Grandpa's trash-talking."

"Then outscore him," she said before leaving.

He did. He kept swishing three-pointers. "Well, you sure got the Hamilton genes," I said.

"Actually, my Dad played a lot with me," he said. "So Whitaker genes."

"You'll win the game tomorrow for sure."

"I'll deserve it if we lose."

I asked him what he'd deserve it for, but he didn't say anything. I told him it was his birthright to win. We went inside and sat in front of the video game console. Since his father ditched out on other parental responsibilities, I figured Terrance hadn't received The Talk.

"So did your Dad ever talk to you about men and women lying with each other?"

"Lying to each other? Yeah, he showed—"

"No, lying *with* each other."

He fiddled with the video game controller. "Kind of."

"What do you mean, 'kind of'?"

"You know. How it works and stuff."

"Before marriage, think like a eunuch. After marriage, think like Solomon."

"But didn't Solomon have thousands of wives?"

"Right. So you have to pay as much attention to your one wife as he did to thousands. See, you'll have it easy. Also, remember to thank God every day for your pecker. If you thank him for it, you're less likely to misuse it. Me, I'm past misusing it. But I'll still die happy."

"I don't want you to die," Terrance said.

"Well, I got more life in me than most." I began the jitterbug, which he didn't recognize but I told him it was a spot-on rendition of the original dance, created by the jazzmeister Cab Calloway. I taught him the moves. He didn't botch it too badly. He taught me the Superman. I'll have to practice the footwork. "I know," I said. "Let's go to the park!"

So Mirabelle and Terrance both got in Ehud's back seat because the front seat was occupied by what Mirabelle called trash but I told her it was actually miscellanea. I pretended I was their chauffeur, dipping the brim of an imaginary cap and calling them Ma'am and Sir in a British accent.

The park disappointed. It had a pond smaller than a puddle of spit and ducks that looked too lazy to migrate. I took out my wallet and waved the last bill from my honorarium. "Twenty dollars to whoever catches a duck first!" That sent the kids running. I rested on a red bench, and soon Mirabelle joined me, swinging her legs. Terrance had torn a long strip of vine from a wall and was fashioning a slipknot.

"Your brother's a smart cookie," I said.

She laughed. "Cookies don't have IQs."

I remembered the first time Catherine and I had an inkling about Mirabelle. She was five, visiting my apartment, and while everyone talked in the kitchen, she pulled a primer on Hebrew from my bookshelf and began to rewrite the letters. When we found her, she'd copied the alphabet twice. I funded lessons up in Portland, and in a year she was reading ancient Hebrew with some fluency. In third grade, she was already doing college math.

"Do your classmates have high IQs?"

"Academy kids were dumb but the new school kids are mean. They twist my hair when I know things they don't."

Catherine hadn't told me she'd taken her out of private school. I was hardly going to endure such mistreatment of my flesh and blood. "Listen carefully." I leaned in conspiratorially. "When people twist your hair, poke them with a pencil." I mimed the action. "Don't worry, it's kosher with God. Eye for an eye, and all that."

She scrunched her face. "If God knows everything, how could he keep everything in his head? It would explode."

A doubting Thomas at her pipsqueak age. I could only imagine the questions she'd be asking in a few years. "Some people think your head should explode, little missy!"

"I can remember lots of things," she said. She stuck a thumb near her mouth, aping a microphone, and rattled off a stream of words: "Did you wash my laundry? I did but you need to pick up the tri-tip from the store. Why isn't the BBQ clean? Because you were too exhausted to scrape it last time." She seemed to be recounting a conversation between her mother and Dennis.

After five minutes without intermission, I interrupted. "Mirabelle, do you do this often?"

"No," she said, in a way that told me the opposite. "Also, do you know? Mom stopped eating when Dad left."

"She does that sometimes," I said. "The trick is to tell her she's beautiful. You'll do that, won't you?" Mirabelle nodded vigorously.

A man with a frizzy shock of hair limped up. From the pocket of his tweed jacket he pulled pieces of white bread and scattered them on the ground. Ducks swarmed. He started rambling on about foreign cities he'd been to, Cairo to Moscow, finally telling a story about visiting a woman in Marienbad only to discover she had a husband. He gave some bread to Mirabelle, who in a solemn, sacramental gesture passed it to the birds. Terrance took advantage of the flock density to lay his vine trap. The man finished and asked, "You ever been to those places?"

"Oh, yes," I said. "Marienbad!" I'd not only visited but had a great story. But when I placed an order for my memory, it was still on the fritz. I tried to divert the topic. "I have these two wonderful grandchildren." Grandchildren were the only currency I had left.

He glanced at the children and offered an obligatory smile. "What about Marienbad?"

At any other point I would have converted this man in a flash. My Marienbad story had converted ten people in Saigon and seven in Bulgaria and hundreds at a tent revival in Kenya. But now I was left with a shadow memory. "It's not that good of a story," I said, and my heart burned with the falsehood.

The duck rose up honking. The red of its mouth gaped large. I shielded my face and Mirabelle, but Terrance yanked on the vine around its foot. Hell's bells, the boy had won himself a twenty! As the duck swung around and attacked Terrance, bill snapping at his face and wings hammering his arms, I expected him to jump away or to pin the bird, but he just took the beating. His eyes were closed, his hands fastened at his sides. His expression scared me. He wasn't grimacing but smiling, as if he deserved the pain.

◆ ◆ ◆

On Saturday morning, I woke up and delivered pugilistic knocks above both ears to dispel the fog, which helped me remember my Wednesday scribblings. The handwriting was hard to read, but the Indonesian story was knock-up, knockdown funny. I laughed uproariously on six and a half occasions, not to mention one knee-slapping moment when an errant dart impaled a penis gourd. It was hilarious for one blooming reason: I didn't remember a word of it.

I knew I'd relived this experience with a wheelbarrow's worth of nostalgia a few nights ago, but the fog was spreading. The Lord giveth and taketh, but at my age, mostly taketh. I hooked suspenders over a plaid shirt onto wool pants and found a note from Catherine. Her slave drivers demanded she toil on a Saturday.

Terrance was hitting buttons on a fake guitar while circles sloped onscreen. I asked him whether he knew how to play real guitar, and he said no, and declined my offer to teach him, which was for the best because I'd never played. I hunted up Mirabelle, and after we built a sandcastle in the backyard representing the tower of Babel, complete with army-men figurines for apostates, we leveled it, swinging and stomping.

By the time Catherine arrived home from work, I was reading a terrifying story to Mirabelle. We'd hung a blanket over the window and closed the door and read by flashlight on the carpet. Mirabelle told me to do the voices like Daddy, so I made every voice different, from the kid to the monsters. Catherine called around the house before opening the door. She looked from me to Mirabelle to the book. "So you're playing the good father now," she said.

We all gathered at the table, where Catherine had dumped a take-out pizza. Catherine snapped at Terrance to quit his video game. The kids weren't bothered that we didn't pray.

"My day was terrible," Catherine said without prompting. She'd already eaten half a sausage slice and was taking three more. She droned on about how they were abusing her and how she only wanted to quit. It seemed to be a complaint in disguise for being abandoned by Dennis, and pity welled up in me. I considered staying longer to help. Terrance snuck a butter knife under the table and, judging by the sound, rapped his knuckles.

"Pop, you're quiet tonight. What's wrong? Lost all your energy?" Catherine ate a piece of sausage that had fled her slice.

"We had an excellent day, didn't we kids?" They refused to look at me.

Catherine glanced at the clock. "Pop, don't you have to get going?" All day my uneasiness about the speech had grown, and now a Son of Anak couldn't have dragged me there.

"I'd prefer to cheerlead for Terrance," I said. "Rah-Rah-Ree. Kick 'em in the knees."

We dropped Mirabelle off for a sleepover at a friend's house, which thrilled Catherine because Mirabelle's social pool was near extinct. "Behave yourself," Catherine told her firmly, before Mirabelle walked in a dignified, adult manner to the front door.

At the gym we dropped Terrance off before Catherine hightailed away.

"There's a space," I said, pointing. "Another. Another. That one looks splendid."

"You're going to go to that meeting," she said, pulling out of the exit.

"What about Terrance's game?"

"You need to keep your obligations." She sped up next to the MAX train.

"I didn't bring my notes."

"Since when have you needed notes?"

"Okay, okay, okay, okay." I tried to negotiate my way around it, but couldn't create an excuse. "So my memory's not as surefooted as before."

"Is that so?" Catherine said. "But you could remember all my schools." She was eyeing me sideways, and I didn't like her tone. After we passed several bikers with their right pant leg rolled up, she pulled into a parking lot, far from the storefront's glow. She drummed the steering wheel with her hands before shutting off the car.

"Pop, what else have you forgotten?"

The failures I remembered. My shortcomings as a father, spending too little time with my wife, working too hard. Regret worked like amber, embalming. But forgotten? All my work over the years. I couldn't remember the names of people I had led to the gates of heaven. Even the country names were growing fuzzy. Certainly I'd forgotten the anecdotes I'd told in hundreds of tented gatherings to loosen up the heart's soil. I knew it wasn't the natural clunkiness of old age, but a punishment. Seems like the good Lord wanted to put me in the humbling room, for all the things making me feel big were gone and all the things making me feel small were lingering.

But I didn't want to spill all that onto my poor daughter. So I hot-wired a smile and said, "How am I supposed to know what I've forgotten?"

She took a deep breath. "Fine. Well. You ever heard this story? A missionary had been evangelizing the Amazonian villages around Manaus. Helped slaughter a chicken, catch a python. But nobody was listening to the white man. One day, three teenagers tried to provoke piranha by dumping chicken blood in the water and daring each other to get in." She was tilting her head and swinging with rhythms. I admired the storytelling ability. Hamilton genes!

"Long story short, one fool of a boy got a finger bit off. Anyway, the missionary went fishing for piranha the next day and caught a mess of them with piranha flesh as bait. But when he slit their bellies to prepare dinner, he found the boy's finger! Though there wasn't a doctor to reattach it within 100 kilometers, he still returned it to the boy. The boy asked, 'How'd you get this?' and the missionary replied, 'Didn't I tell you I was a fisher of men?'"

I laughed hard. "Daughter of mine! Where'd you find that jewel?"

She fell silent and her face crumpled. I didn't see the attack coming because I blinked. She wrapped me up in a wrestler's grip, her arms purchasing a stranglehold around my neck. I couldn't move—she had me pinned against the seat. When I first heard the sound I couldn't recognize it. It sounded like she was trying to hawk up some phlegm. But after I realized she was crying, I reinterpreted her body language. Her embrace was so genuine it made all the previous hugs seem counterfeit.

Then the wires connected in my brain and I knew, from the intensity of her hug, that the story originally belonged to me.

We didn't go to the youth group. Catherine canceled for me by phone. We returned to the gym and divined the past by the scoreboard. They'd been skunked. Suited players slunk from the orifices of the building, bodies limp as effigies. When Terrance emerged from the locker room, he didn't even look at us. "You played wonderfully in the second half," Catherine said.

"I was on the bench the whole second half," he said. "And I didn't deserve to play in the first half." On the ride home, I insisted that next game he'd whip the opponents into his bondservants, but before we reached the house, he said, "Dad came to my games."

Catherine got a call about a problem with Mirabelle. We dropped Terrance at home and drove to the friend's house. The streetlight in front of the house had the deathly glow of a low-battery flashlight. Corrugated curtains blocked off dark windows.

"I'll be back in a second," Catherine said.

"I have experience in exorcisms."

"Pop. Seriously? It's Mirabelle. Please don't. Not now. Just stay in the car."

But I'd already shut the door and was lunging for my toes to warm up.

The mother's cheeks looked eroded by stress. "They're in the backyard," she said, ushering us through the house. A blue tent, lit from within by a solitary bulb, was pitched on the grass beneath the sycamore tree. Even as Catherine and I approached the opened slit, I could hear Mirabelle's drone: "Did you go to her again tonight? You'd miss dinner with your kids because of her? It's not my fault I need to get away from this hellhole. It's miserable here."

Catherine lifted the tent flap and found the woman's daughter lying on her back wearing headphones. Mirabelle sat crosslegged with the flashlight under her chin, and didn't stop speaking when Catherine said her name. I started to duck inside, but Catherine barred the way with an arm. I knew she feared I'd launch into some charismatic mumbo-jumbo. But I gently removed her arm and crawled inside on all fours. Mirabelle didn't look at me or stop: "You never lift a lazy finger around here. Why should I when I have to deal with your attitude? You sicken me, you make me so sick I want to die. " I dipped in close and hugged her hard. "Do you really want the kids to hear you—" Mirabelle surfaced as though she'd just seen me: "Granddaddy. I was waiting for you."

I carried Mirabelle out in my arms, thanking the mother and apologizing as we left. In the car I sat in the back with Mirabelle.

"Honey," Catherine said, looking in the rearview mirror, "you don't have to repeat those conversations anymore." Her voice teetered on a high edge.

"But you told me not to forget him," she said.

"Yes, but—" She gripped the steering wheel. "Yes, right."

In the mirror, Catherine caught my eye, asking for help. "You want to remember your father the right way," I told Mirabelle, and I took her hand and squeezed it. Catherine looked gratefully at me, a look I hadn't seen in years.

In the driveway, Terrance stood in the headlights, shooting hoops. Catherine parked the car near the street so he'd have room to continue. Once we emerged, we all stood there, observing his rotation around the court. The backboard thumped. The net hissed.

"Thanks for watching *now*," he said.

Catherine let Mirabelle sleep with the popsicle-stick cathedral in her room. Through a part in the curtains I watched Terrance shoot. When he made it, he shot again. When he missed it, he pounded the ball against his forehead. Despite the double panes, I could hear the thump of flesh against leather. So I went out and stood under the net, rebounding the ball for him. For once, probably because there wasn't much left in my head, I had enough wisdom to stay silent. He shot, the net or rim spoke, I thrust the ball back. Thankfully, he stopped hitting his head after he missed. We shot and rebounded for a good half hour without a word.

"I'll stay out here as long as you need me," I said. I meant it, too. Nothing but loyalty between Hamiltons. I noticed Catherine watching us from the window. Terrance shot for another spell before we went inside, our skin prickly from the cold. I said, "You shoot like good ole Wilt, you know that?" That tore half a smile out of him.

I went into Catherine's room and sat on her bed. She had curled up with an afghan. "Thank you for your help with the kids tonight," she said.

"I would do it a thousand times over," I said. "Anything for family."

"Anything for family?" she said. She was on the edge of laughter or tears. "Oh, Pop. I wish you'd been losing your memory your whole life."

I hated to admit it, but she was right. Forgetting made me remember what was important. Now I needed to say one important thing, but I couldn't say it without a story. I shuffled through my foggy memory and came up with one, only one.

"Remember that time in Thailand?" I said. "We were taking a break from ministry in—Cambodia? Laos? Somewhere in Southeast Asia. And we went to Thailand, visiting waterfalls? You loved waterfalls. You loved to stomp in the puddles at the bottom and stick out your tongue to catch the mist. At one waterfall, I got you two ice cream cones. You ate them right up. And on the roads back—twisty as a snake!—you got sick. You were greener than the jungle! Head hanging out the window. But you know what you said when we finally reached the bottom of the mountain and got off the minibus? You wanted another ice cream! Your mother and I sure laughed at that one. But I don't know what I was thinking buying you two cones. I was probably trying to make you happy because you were always unhappy after a move." Now I got to the point. "Bad judgment on my part. Just one of my many mistakes. I'm sorry. I'm sorry. I'm sorry."

Catherine had sunk into her thoughts and I couldn't read her.

"Remember that?" I asked.

She smiled sadly. "I can't forget."

Acknowledgments

Big huzzahs to the Soggy Biscuits, my perennially faithful crew who allowed me to crash their writing group so many years ago, and who flogged me onward with cheers, alcohol, writing retreats, and dirty jokes. I couldn't do it without you folks, and I love each of you:

- ·Mindi Combs
- ·Jennifer Carr
- ·Jeff Wallace
- ·Garrett Calcaterra
- ·Eric Tryon
- ·Jonathan Huston

Thanks to the Combs family for writing retreat facilities: their cabin on the Rogue River and the house in Temecula. Inspiration comes in beautiful places, and you've provided that in spades.

Huge thanks to the Community of Writers at Squaw Valley, where I workshopped some of these stories, received invaluable feedback, and "networked" in the hot tub.

Thanks to the professor who made me into a writer: Dr. Jack Simons. You taught me so much, but above all you instilled in me the *desire* to write.

My greatest gratitude to my professors over the years:

- · Gina Nahai, a wonderful mentor for my thesis
- · Judith Freeman, who told me I had what it took
- · Janet Fitch, a great teacher and fount of wisdom
- · T.C. Boyle, for his insight and patience with my 10,000-word stories
- · Emily Jenkins, for not telling me to quit after reading my first novel

Thanks to Vern Glaser and Drew Duncan for being early readers and vocal champions of this book and the ones to come.

Three readers and fellow writers to whom I am very grateful: John DeSimone, Lyle Smith, and Thomas Allbaugh. I'll never forget our wonderful sessions at Millie's.

Thanks to every member of the Jack London House, especially Titus Gee and James Roland, for listening to me read early work and laughing at the funny parts, especially the parts I didn't yet know were funny.

To my wife Amber I owe a great deal, but I'm mostly grateful for two things: for agreeing to marry a fiction writer, and for waiting patiently for years.

Also, a big thanks to Kevin Morgan Watson for seeing the potential in these stories and loving them enough to publish them.

John Matthew Fox has published in *Crazyhorse*, *Third Coast*, *Shenandoah*, and the *Chicago Tribune*. He provides editing services and resources for writers at the literary blog *Bookfox*, which has received mentions from *The Guardian*, *Los Angeles Times*, *Publisher's Weekly*, and *The Huffington Post*. He earned an MFA from the University of Southern California and an MA from New York University, but after teaching at the collegiate level for a decade, he decided to focus on *Bookfox* full time. After traveling to more than forty countries and living in three, he has settled down in Orange County, California, with his wife, twin boys, and six chickens. *I Will Shout Your Name* is his debut collection of short fiction.

CPSIA information can be obtained
at www.ICGtesting.com
Printed in the USA
BVHW071137170321
602767BV00002B/226